SCRAPS

SCRAPS

Written by **Matthew Francis**

Story by **Ryan Nordin & Matthew Francis**

Written by Matthew Francis
Story by Ryan Nordin and Matthew Francis
@matthewfrancisj / @rye_nordin / @scraps_movie

Cover Illustration by Jonathan Kent Adams
Chapter Illustrations by Annika Danenhauer
Contributions by Chance Housley, Sloane Gordon, and Leighton Strom
Editing by Samantha Zaboski

***Scraps* Youtube, *Scraps* Instagram, *Scraps* Tiktok**
- Short Film Trailer, Short Film Soundtrack,
- Short Film Behind-the-Scenes
- Full *Scraps* Short Film

First edition printing, March 31, 2025
Published by Matthew Francis and FrancisFilm, LLC
Printed in the U.S.A. 2025

For Montana, Minnesota, and the romantic
teenage love stories we wish we could have had.

Table of Contents

Chapter 1

Alone in Montana

This view is wasted on me. You'd do so much more with all these colors.

Gus Shepard watched the blue Rocky Mountains and green forested hills glide past his car window. The orange ombre of the lowering sun cast a golden glow over grazing cattle in sloping pastures just beyond the glass. Perennially shy and artistic, Gus always noticed *every* small detail around him: the color palettes of his surroundings, a stranger's intricate body language, and how every subject was framed within the scenery of his gaze. Looking past his own freckles and sandy blond hair in the window, Gus surveyed the familiar wildlife from the safe back seat of his father's red 1969 Chevy Blazer as they sped down the rural road from Bozeman airport. Through the glass, far away, Gus spotted a pair of songbirds skipping from tree to tree. He smiled somberly at their inaudible melodic chirping.

Gus peeled his sight off of the colorful Montana landscape to try and replicate it as just a black-and-white drawing in the timeworn sketchbook on his lap. The *scritch* of his pencil became the

1

only sound inside the tense car as they drove far from town. Like the many sketchbook pages preceding it, this one soon filled with Gus's simple nature sketches, each almost lifelike and untainted. When Gus finished the final intricate flourishes of a sparrow's wing, he signed his name below the drawings and added the date: *June 6, 2003*. From the rearview mirror, Gus's stoic father looked up to watch his son check over his work. Dan Shepard felt no need to break the silence.

Gus lifted his worn sketchbook and flipped the paper around its binding to a fresh page. He looked back through his closed window, lost in a daze. He breathed in his nerves and forced out his fears. The Chevy Blazer turned down a small, winding road, and Gus noticed the weathered *Livingston, Montana* sign he hadn't seen in thirteen years. Amber sunset melted to a purple evening, and no more city lights lit their way. His father's car soon crossed the same old army bridge Gus used to collect frogs under. His head swayed as they bumped over the same train tracks he used to practice balancing on, until finally, he saw it—the secluded log cabin that housed all his childhood memories. After all these years, Gus wondered if the home would still smell like his mother's rosy pink perfume he missed so much. He sighed. Gus shook the thought away.

The Chevy came to a stop in the driveway of his father's quaint cabin surrounded by pine trees. A small flowing creek trickled nearby. Gus stepped out of the car and surveyed the flat, utilitarian property he remembered so well. Beautiful behemoth mountains loomed far off in the distance, so tall they pierced the white clouds above. To Gus's right stood his dad's woodshop with its weathered green sign that read *Shepard's Custom Furniture* hanging above it. The wooden placard was covered in shriveled leaves that blew away in the breeze.

Dan Shepard shut his car door. Gravel crunched beneath his feet as he walked around the rear bumper to meet Gus. The taciturn middle-aged lumberjack looked the boy up and down, still not used to his visiting son's height.

"You've grown a lot, Gus," Dan mumbled as he opened the trunk. "All your stuff is still in your old room."

Gus tried to offer his father a faint smile, but the gesture was lost as the man forged ahead with his suitcase. Dan paused under the dimming yellow porch light and offered a dull, tired nod to his son.

"Get settled. Need you up early to explain the shop," Dan informed him.

Gus nodded. "Yes, sir. Thank you."

He was so exhausted. His bones were heavy.

A familiar warmth eased that burden as Gus entered the home he once knew so well. Not much had changed, yet the heat felt different somehow. He walked through the hallway, passing empty log cabin walls. He stopped and stared at the darker squares of wood amid the otherwise sun-bleached paneling. *When did he take Mom's paintings down?*

He lugged his suitcase up the creaking wooden stairs to his cramped attic bedroom. Gus looked around the space he'd grown up in. Over the past decade, it had become merely excess storage space. Several dusty boxes towered high.

Gus dropped his bags near his childhood bed, which hadn't been touched in ages. It stood perfectly made, ready in case he had ever come to visit. *Did Dad want me here sooner?*

His duvet on the bed was still his old one covered in bucking quarter horses and roaming cowboys. Gus sat down on the spring mattress and absentmindedly placed his sketchbook and leather canvas backpack on the bedside table. But it wasn't his previous end table. It was something different now—a wooden trunk with deep grooves he had never seen before.

Gus scoped out the object, lost on where it could have come from or how his dad had gotten the heavy thing all the way up to his room. He tilted his head in thought. The trunk had a little brass padlock. Gus tugged the lock down, trying to open the hefty wooden box. It did not budge. He shook his head and shrugged, too tired to think any longer. He pulled off his baggy sweater, faded jeans, and sweaty socks, tossing them to the side to deal with in the morning. Gus yawned wide and turned off the lamp near his headboard. After lying down and pulling his sheets over his torso, he drifted to sleep.

Dan's screeching tea kettle and the aromatic allure of freshly roasted coffee beans were a natural alarm that woke Gus up just hours later. The morning sunlight poured onto Gus's soft skin as he rolled over in his boxers. He sat up and rubbed his eyes. Alone in the dusty attic, Gus sighed, remembering this was his new normal.

He slugged down the stairs to join his father in the kitchen. Sunny-side eggs and herbed sausages sizzled in a cast-iron skillet. Gus paused in his steps when he saw their wooden dining table set for two. Only two.

"Hey, kid," Dan grunted as he flipped the eggs onto a plate.

Gus yawned a "Morning" and scraped back an oak chair to take his seat.

Dan placed two plates of fried eggs, crispy sausage links, and buttered toast on the table. He hiked up his overalls before he sat down and poured two cups of coffee from his tin French press: one for himself and one for Gus. Dan took a sip. Coffee caught in his graying beard as he sliced coins of sausage. There was an awkward silence as they both ate their breakfast. Gus hesitantly looked up at his father as he spread huckleberry jam across his toast. They both had been avoiding crucial conversations.

"So. What happened to all of Mom's pictures?" Gus ventured.

Dan glanced up from the brim of his coffee cup. He said nothing.

"Before she... passed..." Gus cleared his throat. "She said you were lonely way out here. She—"

Dan grunted to avoid Gus's reach for connection. The aging man stood up from the table and swung on his Carhartt work jacket.

"Finish up," Dan muttered. "I'm going to the shop."

Gus sighed and turned to watch Dan plod off. He should have known he wasn't going to get much out of his pragmatic father.

"What are we working on today?" Gus called out.

"An oak dining set. Two more chairs to square things up," Dan responded. He grabbed keys off a small hook near the door.

Gus nodded and downed his eggs as his dad pulled on his work boots and exited the cabin. Gus stuffed a last piece of toast into his mouth and followed.

Behind their home sat the large barn that was his father's woodshop. Gus walked inside to see all sorts of carpentry machines for sawing, sanding, and cutting. Wooden boards lay scattered about, dry sawdust clung to every surface, and motes swirled in the sun gleaming through the wide windows. Gus watched his father lift a huge stack of untreated boards and lower them next to his cluttered workbench.

"Summer job starts now." Dan adjusted his overalls and looked down at Gus. "May as well put you to work before you're gone for art college."

Gus nodded with hesitation. He had never used the machines. Before the divorce, before he and his mother moved to Minnesota, he had grown up only playing in the yard outside while his father worked all day. Now, though, no longer too young to operate the equipment, he was determined to learn so he could spend at least a few good months with his distant dad. He'd rather reconcile over woodwork than remain strangers stuck in the same house all summer.

Dan gestured at Gus. "Grab a couple more of those two-by-fours."

Gus turned to the wall that held dozens of variously sized boards on organized shelves. He had no idea which ones were two-by-fours but grabbed a stack.

Dan stopped him. "That's a four-by-four."

Gus put the lumber back and grabbed some skinnier pieces of wood. They were correct. He struggled to lift the heavy boards onto the bench.

Dan measured some oak and marked it in three places. Gus pulled out a little journal to take notes. His dad lined up each piece of wood, trimmed the ends to equal lengths, and tossed the scraps into a bucket near the shop's furnace. Gus quickly learned the ins and outs of the machines as his father demonstrated proper techniques and grunted what mistakes would end in a mangled finger. In total, Dan spoke only a short few sentences over the workday. Gus gleaned his dad felt no need to over-chat, and the constant blare of the machines complicated the chore of catching up anyway. When Gus left for a few moments to collect a new armful of heavy boards, the harsh buzzing from the saw seemed deafening.

"Is it always this loud?" Wincing, Gus placed the boards on the workbench and covered his ears as Dan worked on cutting a detailed edge with a particularly grating jigsaw. Dan didn't hear his son.

"Dad?!" Gus called out.

Still nothing.

Gus tapped Dan's shoulder, and his father lifted one of his protective earcups.

"What?! Sorry. My hearin's bad," he yelled back.

Gus chuckled. "Yeah. No wonder."

The hours passed. Gus mostly shadowed Dan's procedures, ran to retrieve more wood, burned excess scraps in the furnace, or cleaned up behind his father. However, he performed well, and Dan soon let Gus test out the smaller machines himself. Dan steamed and bent the oak as Gus assembled chair pieces. Soon father and son worked side by side, both using electric sanders at the same time.

Dan looked over at Gus periodically, checking his form. Gus knew he did something right when his dad would simply nod, saying nothing. However, it wasn't until Gus was tasked with brushing dark polish onto the smooth wood, revealing its luscious weaving grain, that the first spark of pride in his own carpentry came to him that first day. Polishing, to Gus, felt exactly like painting: each new stroke revealed something beautiful and unexpected.

Toward the end of Gus's first shift, Dan inspected his son's technique as he wiped down the set of finished chairs. Polish stains coated every inch of Gus's painting shirt and overalls. However, as Gus took a step back to let his father appraise his work, Dan nodded his silent approval once again, even offering a rare grin of pride. Gus perked up with satisfaction. Both shoulder to shoulder, Dan nudged Gus with his elbow.

"Good job, kid."

The shop's windows were now dark and starry after the long day. Never one to waste time, Dan handed his son a broom to collect and discard all the wood shavings piled around them. He left Gus alone to clean up as he headed back to the cabin. When the door closed, Gus groaned in the dark silence and started sweeping.

Once inside the cabin, Gus collapsed onto his bed. He was sweaty and covered in sawdust. His body ached. But before getting back up to shower, his eyes drifted to the wooden trunk beside him again. An object was tucked behind it. Intrigued, Gus reached over and pulled out a small framed painting of a bitterroot, Montana's state flower. His chest tightened. It was one of his mom's favorite pieces from long ago. One of *his* favorites.

This one too? Why'd he take it down?

Annoyance flickered through Gus, but he pushed it aside. He was too tired. Standing up, he walked to his wall and hung the artwork carefully on an empty nail and stepped back to enjoy it. The pretty pinkish-purple wildflower was tiny, but somehow it could grow strong within all the dry, rocky soil around it. Gus softened. His mother's bitterroot flower looked perfect on his wall.

Gus's first week went the same as his first day. Breakfast, woodwork, lunch, woodwork, dinner, bed. Only the type of furniture or decorative carpentry piece they created changed as his father received orders from neighbors or people from more distant towns. A couple from Missoula requested small maple bedside tables. A woman from Helena ordered matching walnut boxes for her husband's anniversary gift. Dan was well-known in Montana for his quality furniture. Gus enjoyed witnessing his father's passion in action however non-conversational the man remained. Gus liked the work itself. It passed the time, and he loved finding artistry in whatever way he could find it.

Still, Gus felt more like Dan's employee than his own son. By his first weekend, he itched to see another face. To try something new.

Dan's fork eased through his cheesy omelet as he finished pouring his morning brew. He took a slow satisfying bite of his eggs alone at the dining table. Gus walked through the kitchen, passing his father, and moved along to the front door. He didn't sit down for breakfast. Dan regarded his son suspiciously.

"Where are you going?" Dan asked, leaning to the left to view his son, crouched in the doorway lacing his Nike Blazer high-tops.

Gus took a deep breath before standing up to ask his dad a request. "It's my first day off. I thought I could explore more of Livingston." Gus looked over. "Can I borrow the car?"

Dan paused. He never really took days off. Why bother? There was so much to do. However, he doubted that reasoning would work on an eighteen-year-old.

"Humpfrh," Dan grumbled in return, tossing Gus his keys.

Gus smiled, clearly eager but anxious to go see the town on his own.

"Don't wreck it. Tomorrow we're back in the shop, bright an' early," Dan reminded.

Gus beamed back. "Yes, sir!"

Gus sped through the door and bounded outside.

Dan exhaled a deep long breath as he watched his son race toward the car. Alone at the table, he took a bite of his hash browns and continued eating his breakfast in silence.

Gus twisted the car key to ignite the engine, shifted his father's Chevy into first gear, and sped out of their gravel driveway. As he coasted down the rural roads to Livingston amid wide pastures, tall mountains, and bright skies, Gus found that he was feeling grand.

The glaring sun around a bend soon forced Gus to pull out his sunglasses, cheap but stylish things his mother gave him a few years back. Gus caught his reflection in the rearview mirror. Memories flashed of riding in his mom's dinged-up minivan, recapping his school days and joyously singing along with her to NSYNC and Nelly Furtado. He smiled, soaking up the past. Gus then remembered his grandfather had just sold that minivan to cover funeral costs. His chin fell. He pulled the shades off.

He tried reminding himself that she would have wanted this. She'd have wanted him to explore. Maybe the old shops she took him to in town were still around. Maybe he'd spot the same critters she used to paint during their lazy picnics in the park. He knew this venture into the city wouldn't feel the same alone, but Gus promised himself he'd find the perfect spot to sketch in her honor today. He felt the urge to draw something again after a week away from his sketchbook. He needed it.

Gus boosted the radio louder, trying to psych himself back up. Outside his windows, a few unfamiliar sights passed by: construction workers, chain restaurants, empty parking lots. Soon he found a spot to park and set to walking, passing rotting tree trunks and condo development signs. Strolling through the center of town carrying his sketchbook and canvas backpack, so many forgotten childhood moments rushed back into his mind. Gus decided to window-shop the same stores where he and his mom pretended they could buy toys or artwork, but when he peered into his favorite old-timey candy shop, he found it empty. Out of business. Gus spun a slow circle. The entire street was desolate.

Looking for lunch, Gus was at least relieved to see that Mark's In & Out, the drive-in diner his dad had always loved, still had their footlong chili dogs on the menu. He also ordered a strawberry ice cream cone, his mom's favorite.

Eventually, Gus hiked up to Sacajawea Park and found a familiar bench where he'd often sat with his parents. It had a serene view of the park that relaxed him. He remembered the scenery like he'd seen it just yesterday. As quiet hours passed in that one spot, Gus drew busy passersby, the Yellowstone bridge, and the calm lake surrounded by cottonwood trees. His favorite part of his forming landscape was the two adult geese and their five goslings floating near the pebbled shore right before him. When he finished the final feathers of the little bird family swimming in peace, he finally felt welcomed back to his version of Montana.

Chapter 2

The Rebellious Skater

Evening's hunger told Gus he should probably finish sketching, and he headed back toward the parked Chevy to drive home for dinner. On his way, he heard distant laughter and scratching noises he couldn't quite place. They came from a concrete park he didn't remember from his childhood. As he walked closer, he passed a sign that read *McNair Skatepark*. Gus had never heard of it. The park had smooth, sloping concrete mounds, wells, and ramps that rose high above his vantage point. Various cliques of kids and teenagers loitered around.

Curious, Gus stopped to peer through the chain-link fence for a better look and witnessed a strange world. Shirtless, sunburnt teenage boys with baggy shorts rode skateboards up and down steep ramps. The skaters passed joints and chugged beers while vibing to music playing from a boombox. Pretty girls with silky hair and ripped jean skirts sat on the edges of the park, smoking cigarettes and chatting. Several skaters followed each other in a line around

11

connecting wavy concrete bowls. Three boys attempted to skate on a flat railing. Only one of them succeeded, and when the other two wiped out, the guys all howled in laughter together.

Gus's eyebrows raised. It was a ridiculous sort of impressive, the gutsy tricks the skaters could pull off with just a simple wooden board beneath their feet. One particular boy around Gus's age had messy dark hair, strong muscles, loose ripped jeans, and a red shirt with cut-off sleeves. He downed a Hamm's beer, crushed it against his skull, tossed the empty can, and stuck out his tongue in pure joy. He was... brazen. The rebellious boy grabbed his skateboard, slid down into the bowl, and shot up the concrete lip into the sky. Flying like an eagle above Gus and all the other skaters, he bent his torso to briefly grab his board mid-air, and then twisted back until he faced his crew below as the board flipped under his feet. Gus's jaw lowered by itself. The boy landed back on his board effortlessly and smoothly glided back down the side of the bowl with a yelp born of adrenaline.

"Hell yeah, Bridger!" one of the riders called out to the boy as the rest of the skaters slapped their boards against the concrete, applauding him. Bridger zoomed to a stop.

Gus, dazzled, caught himself beaming as wide as the other skaters. He felt drawn to their group even though he was yards away, hidden behind a fence. One of the older boys of the skate crew turned aimlessly away from the group and spotted Gus. This snapped Gus from his admiring trance. The taller, rough-looking guy squinted at him curiously, almost suspiciously. Gus turned his head away in embarrassment and snuck away from the fence.

Later that night, under the desk light in his attic bedroom, Gus coughed as he dusted off a years-old Apple computer his dad had been storing in his room. The dial-up finally connected and Gus launched Internet Explorer. He typed "skateboarding" into the search engine. Gus scrolled through pictures of pro riders, read skateboarding articles, and watched choppy videos of trick demos. There was so much Gus didn't know. He wanted to absorb all he could, but he soon stopped on an image of a young professional skater hitting a rail. The man was handsome... and shirtless. His torso dripped with sweat under a harsh sun in various action shots of him showcasing classic skate tricks. Gus lingered on the final photo, in which the young man posed for a skateboarding magazine. The man held his skateboard in his arms and flashed a dashing smile. He looked like a slightly older version of that wild skater boy from the park.

Gus lost himself in the picture. In all his art classes growing up, he always struggled with reconstructing the human form. These curving and twisting tricks achieved with only body and board were so fascinatingly different from anything Gus had seen before that he couldn't help but analyze every swerving curve of this man's muscles. He liked how the sides of his torso elongated, how the bulk of his bare shoulders created traceable lines. The poses the skater could strike *were* art. He loved it.

Gus straightened up awkwardly—he had never stared at a shirtless man without feeling like he'd be caught—but then leaned back in. Alluring aesthetics like these had always grabbed him. He just wanted to analyze the man's form, that's it. Gus zoomed in on the picture.

Out of nowhere, a pixelated pop-up materialized, a voice blurting out, "LOOKING FOR SEXY GIRLS NEAR YOU?!" A photo of a woman with big hair and wearing a wet bikini bounced around on Gus's screen. His head sprang back in shock. Disturbing female moaning erupted from the speaker and Gus fell out of his chair in his rush to tear the cord from his computer. He ripped the wire out and the small speaker fell to the ground. The room went quiet.

"Everything okay up there?" his father called from downstairs.

"ALL GOOD!!!" Gus yelled back, wishing he could evaporate.

Silence was all he heard in return. Gus prayed his father wouldn't come up to his room. After awkward seconds that felt like years, Gus realized his dad had gone back to bed. His hearing *was* terrible. Gus sighed in relief.

That whole week, Gus couldn't stop thinking about skateboarding. His next day off, he searched for any sort of skate store in town. It wasn't until evening that he found what must have been the only one in Livingston. It was called Damage Boardshop. Gus pushed open the glass doors and peered around the space. It was a bit run-down and there were no other shoppers. However, rows and rows of colorful wheelless skateboards with excitingly intricate designs hung from the walls. Gus's eyebrows raised. He didn't know where to start.

A plump and tired middle-aged woman with poorly applied makeup sat behind the counter. She flipped through an outdated fashion magazine while uncoiling a long strip of Hubba Bubba to put in her mouth. She did not look eager to engage with Gus. In fact, it seemed like she wanted him to leave.

Gus lingered, bobbing his head to the store's ambient 90s muzak, admiring each and every skate deck. He stared at the merchandise for much too long and was being much too quiet. The woman glanced up, smacking her gum, and gawked at Gus. She looked confused about what he wanted or how to help him. She angled her face toward a back room.

"Hey Max...? Max!" the middle-aged woman called out. "You back there? I need you up front."

There was no response. Gus glanced at the woman. She smiled in a feigned customer service way, then got up from her slanted chair and disappeared into the back.

Crashing sounds from a video game blasted as the woman entered the messy employees room of her skate shop. She immediately sighed with discontent at the empty beer bottles and food wrappers that cluttered the space. Her gruff, wifebeater-wearing son, Max Stevens, had a skateboard on his lap and was playing *Tony Hawk's Pro Skater 4* on Xbox. To his left sat his best friend, Bridger Owens.

The woman knocked on the wall to grab her son's attention. "Max, you're twenty-two. Can you stop with the damn games?"

Bridger turned, but Max ignored his mother.

"I need your help with a kid out there," his mother urged.

"Tell your new *boyfriend* to do it," Max snarked back.

"Don't start," she replied. "Jay's busy."

"Yeah. Fat ass is busy eating our food and stainin' our couch," Max said, still gaming.

"What was that?" Max's mom huffed, grabbed the remote off the cluttered coffee table, and turned off the TV.

Max whipped toward her. "What the fuck!" He groaned and rolled his eyes.

Bridger eyed the agitated Max and grimaced awkwardly. He wanted to escape the room. "I'll... meet you at the park, dude."

Max leaned his head back and sighed. He held up his arm. Bridger dapped him up, then headed out the back room and toward the front.

Max's mom gestured out to where the customer waited. "Go out there."

"Fuck! Fine. But I'm leaving right after." Max stood up and returned the board on his lap to its place of honor on a side console. It sat next to an old framed image of his father posing with champion skater Rodney Mullen. The high-quality skateboard, signed with Sharpie, read: *To my little pro boarder. —Dad*.

As Bridger sped through Damage Boardshop's storefront, he breezed past Gus, who was still perusing merchandise around the corner. A bell chimed as Bridger exited the front door, but Gus was too busy lifting a shiny bright red deck off the wall to notice the sound. The board he held was firm, strong, and bold. Gus smiled as he inspected the craftsmanship of its smooth edges that he knew his father would have appreciated. However, when seeing the $150 price sticker on the board's base, his eyes fell. The small amount of money he was making from working in his dad's shop was supposed to go toward college. He could never spend that much, especially not on a hobby he didn't even know he could do. Gus placed the board gently back on its shelf. He crossed his arms.

A new person walked into the room from the back. Gus turned. The tall, strong Max Stevens dropped into the chair behind the counter. Gus noticed a bruise on the young man's shoulder before he pulled out a light jacket to throw over his wifebeater. Max squinted at the scrawny Gus. Gus looked away.

"Looking for anything specific?" Max questioned him. "We're about to close."

"A skateboard?" Gus replied, glancing back at Max.

"No shit. They're all around you," Max scoffed, smirking.

Gus smiled through a wince from the casual swearing as Max chuckled.

"Anything cheaper?" he asked, pointing to the red deck.

"No. We only carry the best. We got maple completes for a hundred a pop, Santa Cruz customs for two…"

"Um…" Gus looked down in thought.

Max sighed in annoyance. "If you want cheap, make one yourself."

Gus's head snapped up. "How?"

"I don't know, man," Max said, getting bored. "Glue some wood together or something."

Gus's eyes brightened with an idea, but before he had time to think deeper, the door clattered open and the bell jingled. An older bald man with a beer belly stormed inside, his attitude menacing. Gus watched Max lock eyes with the surly guy. His dull smile dropped to a glare and he straightened his spine as the man approached him.

"What are *you* doing here?" Max asked.

"Where's your mom?" the man returned bluntly.

"She'll be at the house soon."

The man ignored Max and brushed past the front counter to head to the back room.

"Peaches! Baby! You back there?" the man called out.

Max glared back at Gus. "You gonna buy somethin' or what?"

"Sorry… no." Gus slowly backed away and walked out of the store's glass doors with another bell jingle.

Max groaned with irritation in the ensuing silence.

He locked the register, grabbed his own beat-up everyday board, and flipped their door sign to *Closed*. Max shook his head as he exited the shop. He tossed the board under his feet and skated down the sidewalk to join his awaiting crew at the skatepark.

Gus powered up his old computer at home again, but this time he ensured the volume was fully turned off. Into the computer, he typed: "How to build a skateboard?" As the light blue screen reflected against his face, Gus scrolled through steps that explained gluing wood scraps together, then molding, drying, cutting, sanding, polishing, and painting a skateboard deck. He stopped on an image showing trucks, wheels, and grip tape. Gus huffed quietly. How much would all that cost?

Gus returned to Damage Boardshop the next day. Max was nowhere to be found. He approached the front counter hesitantly as Max's mom, Peaches, snapped a bubble with her gum and collected herself.

"Hi," Gus greeted. "Do you have just... trucks and wheels?"

"Yes. My husband was the skateboard expert," the woman said, cocking her head, "but I do still know what wheels are. They're right there."

She pointed down at the glass counter display between them. The clear container inside it held various tools and shiny colored wheels. The many vibrant options overwhelmed Gus, but he was even more discouraged by the high prices. He sighed.

"What could I get with this?" Gus asked slowly. He set a few bills and some change on the counter—about twenty dollars' worth.

"Nothing out here," Peaches replied, then tapped her chin. "Hang on a sec."

The woman stood up and reached around a nearby wall to pull out an old cardboard box labeled *The Carnage Bin*. The box was full of outdated, overly used trucks and wheels that looked like they should have been thrown out years ago.

"My son doesn't want us to sell old parts, but I'll take what we can get..." The woman sighed lightly. "Might be some gems in here that aren't too banged up."

Gus fished through the dingy box until he found a set of rusty silver trucks. Maybe with a bit of steel wool and polish, they'd look okay. He then plucked out a matching set of scratched, faded green wheels. Gus beamed.

"I'll take these," he said. Remembering the webpage's list, he also grabbed a roll of grip tape off a nearby rack. "This too."

The woman rang up Gus's purchases and placed them in a re-used white plastic bag from the grocery shop down the street. As Gus left her store, she watched him doubtfully and snapped her bubble gum again.

Back at the cabin that night, Gus snuck into his father's woodshop with his newly purchased items. He peeked around to ensure his dad wasn't inside. He opened a back closet where he had already stashed a small stolen pile of his father's wood scraps that he'd rescued from the burn bin that morning. Placing his bag of parts behind the scraps, he shut the closet door quietly.

As the next few work days followed, Gus paid extra close attention to how his father used an electric handsaw and motorized sander, to his careful way of brushing on wood polish. Gus always offered to burn their accumulating wood scraps, and whenever Dan was out of sight, he stashed a selection of them in the closet. Soon he had collected the best lumber scraps, leftover sanding strips, a half-empty glue bottle, a mostly full polish jar, fraying brushes, and extraneous paint—everything Gus could finagle together to give himself the best shot at building his own skateboard.

Two weeks after his first visit to the park, late after midnight, Gus tiptoed down from his bedroom to the living room. Like many other evenings, his father had fallen asleep on the couch watching *The Red Green Show*. Dan was snoring so loudly, Gus knew not even the noisy woodshop machines would wake him. He had the rest of the night to himself. He snuck behind his father through the living room and quietly put on his shoes. Gus glanced back at his sleeping father, then swiped the woodshop keys from their hook and exited the cabin.

Gus dropped all his secret supplies on their main worktable and pulled the string of an overhead lamp. On butcher paper, he drew a blueprint for his board. He messed up a few times, redoing the outline until it felt perfect.

Gus grabbed a thick, long block of pine from his scrap bucket, lined it up on the bandsaw table, and began to cut out a mold. He cursed after sawing too far into the lumber. He stopped and listened, hoping his father hadn't heard him or the machine. He grabbed a new wood piece and started again, this time getting it right. Once he'd put together and sanded his mold, Gus ran several pieces of pine through the bandsaw until he had a pile of flat sheets. He brushed wood glue on each and grouped them together. Gus then laid the sheets on the mold and used clamps to tighten down the layers. He hid the entire thing back in his closet to dry, covering it with a dirty tarp so his father would not find it. Gus shut the closet door.

The next morning, Dan peacefully whistled as he flipped over a bubbling blueberry pancake in a skillet. Gus poured maple syrup all over his own stack and scarfed down his first bites of breakfast, seemingly in a rush to start woodworking. As he tasted the pancakes, Gus sighed with delight.

"How is everything you cook so delicious?" Gus asked his father.

"Well," Dan chuckled, "it's nice to finally have someone to cook for again." He sat down with his own plate, a rare smile full of old memories growing on his face. He looked at Gus glowing with hungry energy and started to reminisce.

"You know, back when your mom and I first moved out here, we always—"

"Meet you in the shop!" Gus shot up from the table and placed his syrupy dish in the sink. Dan's eyes widened as he watched his son leave the room to put his boots on. He had never seen Gus this eager to start work. When the door shut and Gus ran off to the woodshop, Dan was left in complete silence. This somehow felt familiar. All alone in the kitchen again, Dan sighed, falling deep into thought.

He pulled out his wallet from his back pocket and flipped it open to the faded image he always kept in the folded leather, the small one of him with Gus's mother, Megan. The photo showed them in their mid-twenties, long before the divorce. They both stood outside this same cabin with beaming faces, joyful new homeowners. They were newlyweds—young, happy, in love. A year later, Gus was born. Dan turned away from the photo and frowned. He felt lost. So many haunting memories were creeping back these days. He grunted as he shoved his wallet back into his jeans, then took another bite of his sweet pancakes and bacon. Dan was in no rush. He shook his head, trying not to think of the days when he always cooked for three.

Dan and Gus quickly moved through the workday, passing tools and handing off tasks, now an efficient team. Even though he was accomplishing all that his father asked of him, Gus had his mind elsewhere. He couldn't stop himself from counting down the hours until he could check back on his skateboard and finish it.

Well into the dark of that night, his father was again sound asleep and Gus took out the now-dry wood from the closet. He knew cutting such a precise shape would be extremely challenging, and it would probably come out looking far unlike what he saw back at the board shop, but he had to try. Gus drew the nose and tail of a skateboard deck on the dry glued wood. Using the skills he learned from his dad, he started cutting out the shape with the bandsaw. He drifted off his saw line, cursed, and course-corrected. After, Gus sanded down the crooked edge and blew off the shavings. It looked smooth and even. He smiled.

Finally, he polished the board to show the fine grain and soon had a clean, thin skateboard deck.

Not far from the shop, Gus placed the fresh skateboard on the old railroad ties and stepped on it to test its durability. He tilted his head down to inspect the wood. Everything looked right. He nodded. Gus then jumped up and down for some added weight. The board snapped immediately.

"Fuck."

His head fell back in frustrated defeat.

Friday afternoon, Gus and his father loaded a redwood table into the truck bed of their customer, Mr. Maven.

"There. She's all set," Dan said, stepping back as Gus hopped down from the truck. Mr. Maven provided payment to Dan, and the two men shook hands.

Mr. Maven then looked over to Gus and smiled. "Glad to see Dan finally has some extra hands around here."

Gus nodded in response. "Thanks, sir."

After their customer drove away, Gus and Dan returned to the woodshop and took off their work gloves. Gus sat down to drink some water as his father went to his desk and filed some paperwork. When he walked back to Gus's side, Dan handed Gus an envelope of cash.

"Your first payment. Plus a small tip from Mr. Maven. You're doing good, kid," Dan stated.

Gus smiled and accepted the envelope, then sighed. "Why's college so expensive?"

"Beats me. I never went. No one in our family has," Dan replied. He nodded at Gus with a hesitant smile. His face then turned serious. "Keep working hard, Gus. Don't get... distracted," he said sternly as he looked Gus in the eye. "You could end up the first of our family with a degree."

Gus breathed in that added pressure and raised his eyebrows. He didn't know what to say.

Distracted by what? Does he know?

Dan patted Gus on the shoulder stoically and walked out of the woodshop.

Left alone, Gus stood still. He was torn between what his father expected of him and what he was thinking—*building*—in secret. His eyes glazed over. Art college had felt so far away before this summer. Now he only had three months left...

Gus drooped his head. The sudden obvious weight of his family's hopes hung heavy. Maybe the skating idea was stupid. *Dad's gonna think I'm lying to him...*

However, as Gus opened his eyes, his head still hanging low, he spotted the bucket of scraps leftover from the day's carpentry. It was all perfectly good wood he could use to re-attempt a homemade board. Gus cringed at the thought. He pushed the bucket under a side table to hide it from his view.

With a guilty, quiet groan, Gus debated with himself for a moment. He watched his diligent father through the window as the aging man walked off into the cabin. Gus hated all this secrecy.

But I can't tell him. He'd never let me do it.

Gus huffed. He leaned down and picked up the scraps bucket and stashed it in his secret closet.

Gus used his next day off to de-stress and get out of the woodshop. He couldn't resist driving by the skatepark again and parked near the sidelines, just like last time. He sat at one of the picnic tables and sketched the park's cottonwood tree again but from a new angle. Gus had hoped he'd have enough courage to enter the mix of all the local teens and finally meet some potential friends here in town, but he just couldn't do it. Without a skateboard, he'd look like a weirdo.

Gus stood up and leaned against the far-off fence, watching the skaters pass back and forth in the concrete bowls. He spotted the gruff older kid from the skate shop and the daredevil Bridger along with a few boys he recognized from last time. Did they hang out here every day? Gus never had a group like this. He sort of wished he had.

Suddenly, Max lunged to pull off Bridger's snapback. Bridger whipped around trying to swipe the hat back, but his older friend lifted it out of reach. Max then ripped off his own cap and threw both to the ground.

"Hat Match!" Max blurted out.

All the boys quickly hooted with bravado and formed a circle around Max and Bridger.

Gus squinted, confused.

One of the skaters, Coop, stepped forward to moderate. He raised his arm, ready to signal. "No limits?"

"No limits," Max confirmed, grinning sneakily at Bridger.

"...shit." Bridger chuckled as he crouched down, hands on knees, prepared to play.

"*GO!*" Coop hollered, driving his hand down as if he held a checkered race flag.

Max and Bridger both dove for the other's hat. The two tussled violently, ripping, pulling, and wrestling each other away from their trophies on the ground. All the other boys watched every swerve and maneuver. Gus, stunned by the savage display, couldn't stop watching. He had never seen a game so chaotic. The rest of the boys cheered over the mayhem, choosing sides. After a few stretched seconds, Max pinned Bridger down and climbed onto his chest to straddle him. Bridger struggled to escape.

"Yeah! You like that?" Max taunted, looking down at Bridger beneath his pelvis.

"Get off!" Bridger tried to wrangle his way out as Max continued to boast his strength for all the other boys surrounding them.

Max leaned down close to Bridger's reddening face. "C'mon, Bridge. Never let them see you weak," he whispered through grimaced teeth.

Bridger pulled one arm free, trying to escape the grapple, but Max caught the arm and pinned it down again. Max turned to his crew, gleefully smirking, as Bridger tried to thrust him off.

"YEEHAW!" Max exclaimed, riding Bridger like a bucking horse. "We got a wild one, boys!"

All the guys in the skate crew laughed as they stepped in closer. Max then elbowed Bridger hard in the side, flipped him over, and pressed Bridger's face against his own hat. Gus's eyes darted to Coop, who gestured to Max as the winner. All the boys whooped and hollered. Max gloated in victory as he got off Bridger's back. Another boy, Avery, lit a blunt and puffed smoke. He chuckled at Bridger, who was rolling around groaning from his loss.

"He got you good, Bridge," Avery chuckled.

Bridger winced, catching his breath. "I think I broke a rib."

"You wanna hit this?" Avery offered, leaning down.

Bridger reached for the blunt and took a rip while lying on the concrete. "Best medicine," he coughed out.

I gotta impress them, Gus thought. *Something legit.* They wouldn't let him hang for no reason, and there was no way they'd teach him how to skate without his own board. They'd never share. He was going to have to teach himself first. Like he always did.

Gus turned to leave, determined to put the scraps from earlier to good use.

A few days later, Gus repeated all his same carpentry steps to build his homemade deck again. His aim was to build this board thicker than the last. The night after the deck mold finished drying, Gus recut, resanded, and repolished the denser board. It was almost sunrise when he finally got to a place where he could test the skateboard on the railroad ties again. Gus took a deep breath and jumped up and down on the piece multiple times. He beamed when the board stayed strong. He picked up the better board and looked it up and down for cracks. There were none. Gus smiled with satisfaction.

While listening to Nickelback on his MP3 player in his room, Gus penciled a mountain scene on the bottom of his skateboard. He referenced the landscape he'd drawn in his sketchbook on his first day back in Montana. He strayed with his pencil, erased the error, and fixed it with a fresh line. This was why he never started with ink.

Later on, Gus changed into one of his older shirts that he didn't mind dirtying. He mixed and arranged small bowls of leftover paints that his dad had instructed him to throw away over the past few days. He didn't have all the colors his mom had used in her old art studio, but Gus was good at making do with little. He swept the brush in careful strokes, watching the muted colors slowly cover the penciled mountain-themed graphic. He let the wet paint dry and then screwed in the cleaned silver trucks on each end of the board. They were still a bit scuffed up, but Gus could tell the trucks were built to last. The faded green wheels he popped on brought the colored graphic together. Gus peeled the grip tape from its plastic and laid it down over the board's top surface. He pressed it to fit and trimmed the excess. That was it.

Gus smiled. It was finished.

He turned the board over under the lamplight to view its construction and final aesthetic. It wasn't perfect, but it was impressive. More than that, it was all his own.

Proud as he was, as he gazed at the skateboard's painted mountain range, he shook his head in doubt. Gus knew it wasn't enough. Not yet. He still had no idea how to use the board. All this work would be for nothing if he couldn't actually skate.

Chapter 3

The Deal

Gus sat alone in the dewy grass drawing under a cottonwood tree at McNair Skatepark. He'd woken up extra early to claim a safe spot before anyone else could arrive. This was the closest he'd ever gotten to the park's concrete slopes. Gus kept his head down, only sketching, as the local skate kids trickled in throughout the morning. Max, Bridger, and their friends showed up around midday. Gus's nervously shaking foot bounced against his homemade board—hidden and unused—beneath his sketchbook. He watched the group of cool skaters as they landed tricks and joked around, wishing he knew the smoothest way to join them. The familiar clang of trucks hitting rails, wheels rolling on concrete, and conversations melding together swirled around the busy park. Gus sketched each intricate detail of the scene before him as he admired it: the fist bump between two baggy-shirted riders, the wolf graphic adorning the underside of a skateboard as it was kicked up and caught, the smoke drifting from joints passed between pretty girls gossiping on the bowl's edge. The

25

multiple crews of skaters spanned vastly different ages, but all exuded the same adrenaline from the thrill of the risk. That raw energy rippled toward Gus as cottonwood tufts floated gently past like a rare flurry of summer snow.

The handsome boy, Bridger, cracked a clever quip that sent everyone laughing as he finished a skate line. In response, Max punched him in the arm.

"Okay, okay. Not bad, Bridge," Max commented. "My turn."

Max dropped his board, pushed off, and laced together several tricks, showing off his impressive skills. All of his friends called out encouragement until he finished by landing what Gus recognized from online demos as a kickflip out of a boardslide on a flat rail. Gus's eyes widened with awe. The boys applauded the smug and talented Max.

Hearing approaching footsteps, Gus turned to his left. Three girls walked his way, and he accidentally locked eyes with the center one. The beautiful, confident girl had flowing curly black hair spilling out from beneath a bright red snapback. She oozed a natural swagger that made Gus tilt his head. Her face had no makeup but donned a captivating smile. She held her own skateboard and wore army capris with a tank top and a little gem necklace. When the girl clocked Gus's gaze, she nodded a casual greeting. Gus smiled back awkwardly. The girl stopped walking and chuckled in a bro-y way. She nodded at Gus's sketchbook, looking down to observe it.

"Hey. Great drawing," the skater girl told him.

"Oh. Thanks," Gus responded, barely looking at her.

"You new here?" she asked.

"Um, yeah." Gus cringed. "You can tell?"

"Collared shirt, those pants...? Yup." The girl smirked.

Gus's attention drifted past the confident girl back to the boys. He resumed his sketch.

The skater girl rolled her eyes. "Don't bother with those idiots. Between them all, they share about two and a half brain cells."

Gus didn't move his eyes from his sketch, too shocked by this girl's bluntness, by how bold and carefree she seemed. He wished he was like her. Gus promptly lifted his head, realizing that maybe she could be the one to teach him how to skate, but she had already walked far off with her two friends. She passed the group of skater boys Gus was drawing.

"Yo, Tara! Lookin' good with those knockers!" one skater cat-called.

Two boys behind him cupped their hands at their chests. The skater girl, Tara, rolled her eyes and flipped them off, barely affect-ed. She skated away, leading her friends through the park. As Tara pumped her legs to speed around a bowl, Max's head followed her zooming path across the concrete, watching her longer than the rest. The hooting boys pulled his focus back to Bridger, who traced a new line. Bridger effortlessly Smith grinded the flat rail and landed a few other small tricks, once again amazing Gus. However, when Bridger followed up by attempting a boardslide on the same rail, he botched the landing and rolled to the ground.

"That was some pussy shit," Max scoffed jokingly. "Quit skat-ing like a faggot."

The guys laughed as Bridger got up and jogged to grab his roll-ing board. He seemed perfectly fine, unfazed by the taunting. Gus, however, was grateful he was sitting far away.

Two older boys walked past Gus to get water and scanned him and his journal suspiciously. They knew he was out of place. Gus looked down at his drawings in embarrassment, covering his journal pages with his hands. Feeling more eyes turning to spy on him, he slammed his sketchbook shut and stuffed it into his backpack.

Gus didn't want to leave the park—he had promised himself he'd skate today—but there was no way he could sit here any lon-ger. He picked up his backpack and snuck to his dad's truck at the very far edge of the parking lot. Once inside, Gus shut the door and dropped his head back against the driver's headrest. He sighed in defeat.

Max Stevens loved days like this. Hot summer afternoons sweating and skating with his boys. They were all he really understood these days. This was his kingdom. He'd be damned to let anything or any-one take it from him. However, today felt off. Something was different.

A familiar lighthearted snicker made him twist his head. Tara, chatting with Sophia and Kelly.

Why is she here?

He watched her mount her board and zip past. He turned as Tara skated by him again without even a glance his way. A sinking in his stomach returned that he hated to remember. She hadn't come to skate since the previous summer.

I knew she couldn't leave it. Not even skating with her college friends can beat skating with me.

But... she wasn't skating with him.

Max needed to know why.

A loud *clank* from Bridger's attempt at grinding a rail pulled Max's attention away from Tara and onto Bridger's line. Bridge had been getting good lately. *Too good.* A bead of sweat rolled down Max's forehead. His determined, unblinking gaze followed the blurred outline of Bridger Owens shooting off a lip into the air to try a tail grab. He bailed before he landed, losing his board and having to chase after it down the bowl.

In the heat, Bridger took off his shirt and drank from his plastic squeeze bottle, letting some of the water trickle down his chest to cool his skin in the hot sun. Max's eyebrows lifted as the glinting liquid slowly dripped down Bridger's sculpted torso. He had been friends with Bridger for years, but lately, Bridger seemed... stronger. His closest friend, his partner in crime, his bro was looking different. Max turned to keep his friend's form in sight, watching the svelte muscles of Bridger's slender back ripple as he kicked alongside his board to go faster and propel himself around the bowl. Max squinted at the shape of him in the distance. As Bridger sped back toward where Max was posted up in the center of the concrete, Max's gaze slowly lowered to notice the bulge in Bridger's jeans. He saw how it swerved as Bridger swerved.

"Max, you're up!" Bridger called to him. Max warped back to reality—back to being outside with others around.

Fuck! These little twerps who kept crashing his skate practices with Bridger always watched him like a herd of sheep. *I can't slip up. No shit like that.* Max snapped back into focus.

Shaking his thoughts away, Max raced down the concrete. "Watch this, dude. You still can't beat me. Never will."

He smirked slyly as Bridger laughed and kicked up his board to rest. Max's eyes narrowed in concentration as he pushed faster toward the largest bowl, popping over the coping at the edge and dropping in. His next move had to be epic. A frontside 360 with an Indy grab? Yeah. That'd do it.

Max flew into the sky. His right hand reached around his back leg to grab the middle of his board as he arched his spine and bent his knees to do a full rotation in mid-air. The entire crew roared as Max landed the move. He smoothly skated back to a huddle of smacking boards. As they slapped his shoulders and bumped his fist, Max grinned, unbeaten as always.

"Top that, choads!" Max gloated with a proud sneer.

The sun set, and the sky of McNair Skatepark deepened into a smokey violet before Gus, who still sat alone in his father's Chevy at the edge of the parking lot. He wanted to finish drawing the final details of his new sketches from today, but it was growing too dark to see. That marked the second goal he hadn't met today. Gus glanced down at his painted skateboard, lying uselessly in the passenger seat beside him, and tossed his sketchbook next to it.

He let out a long sigh and pulled out the keys to the Chevy, fortified for the long drive back to the cabin. However, hoots and hollers drew his attention back to the skatepark. Gus looked up and saw Bridger calling out goodbye to his friends and hopping on his board to skate home. Max and the rest of their crew piled into the back of a blue pickup to drive away. The overindulgent rev of the engine and the boys' raucous banging on the truck's side panels was loud enough to alert the whole neighborhood. Gus watched the boys, wild and free, depart. As the echoes of teenage laughter and the truck peeling away faded, Gus realized he was the absolute last car in the lot. The skatepark was finally empty. This was his only chance.

At last, under the flicker of a lone sodium vapor streetlamp, Gus walked out onto the concrete for the very first time. Free of any judgment, he placed his homemade board slowly on the ground and stepped on it. He felt shaky. Gus pushed off, determined to skate well, but he instantly regretted doing too much. Wobbling back and forth, trying to hold his balance, he feared falling and immediately jumped off the too-fast board, letting it shoot off and roll far away. He raced after it to attempt again, this time at a slower pace.

All he wanted to do was skate in a straight line, but it was impossible. He kept screwing it up. Gus huffed and pushed off with more force on his next attempt, hoping the momentum would help and thinking this time he'd be prepared for the speed. He fell hard on the cold ground. Groaning, Gus got back to his feet. His body ached but he kept at it. Again and again, Gus's lack of balance and refusal to give up led to him kissing the concrete multiple times. One overly ambitious attempt threw Gus sprawling onto his back in a painful wreck. He rolled over onto his stomach, cursing at himself. Concrete dust stung his nose, and his every muscle tightened with soreness. There on the ground, he let his hopes die. Skateboarding just wasn't meant for him.

"Holy shit. You okay?" a smooth voice asked from somewhere behind him. "Here, let me help you up."

Lying there disoriented, Gus turned his neck to find a hand extended out to him. He realized the hand belonged to the daredevil skater he had been watching all week.

Bridger.

The attractive boy, wearing stonewashed Levi's and a plain white tee, was lit in glorious moonlight. Gus didn't know what to do. He was too flustered to speak.

"I... uh..." Gus let out.

"No worries, man. We all fall. I crashed into a tree my first ride." Bridger chuckled as he reemphasized his lowered hand reaching out to help. Gus placed his hand in Bridger's and was rocketed to his feet.

"Why are you skating in the dark?" Bridger chirped with curiosity.

"Oh! I, uh, just wanted to practice by myself," Gus shared. "Why are you here so late?"

"Forgot my MP3 on the bench." Bridger shrugged as, with a SanDisk clutched in hand, he pointed his thumb behind him toward the edge of the concrete.

Gus nodded.

"Whoa! Killer board! Where'd you get it?" Bridger gushed, looking down at Gus's wooden contraption where it had flipped over next to him.

Gus, too, glanced at the makeshift board and blushed. Bridger grabbed it and inspected the deck closely. Its hand-painted graphic glistened in the light of the skatepark's lone streetlamp.

"I made it," Gus admitted timidly.

"You *made* this?" Bridger's eyes gleamed as he looked back at Gus. "Dude, this is sick!"

Gus chuckled. "Thanks. My dad has a woodshop."

"Can I try it out?" Bridger lowered the board, not waiting for an answer.

"Uh, sure, but I haven't really tested"—Gus watched Bridger take off—"it."

It was a near-perfect display of skateboarding under the moonlight. Bridger rode around the bowl, hit a rail, and skated back, sliding to a stop near Gus. He finished with a heelflip in place, then kicked up the board to hold it once again. He marveled at the mountains Gus had painted on the deck.

"This setup is fucking amazing, man." Bridger gestured with delight. "What's your name?"

Gus rubbed the back of his head. "I'm Gus."

"Bridger," the boy responded, reaching for a slap-grab handshake.

Gus paused before linking hands with Bridger. The skater tried to turn the shake into a multi-part dap-up, but Gus flubbed the move. Both boys met eyes. Bridger chuckled and Gus smiled.

"How'd you learn to skate so well?" Gus asked.

Bridger smirked. "From my crew. You should come hang during the day. There are some great riders."

"Oh." Gus shook his head. "I'm not very good. Only starting."

"Right." Bridger squinted. "I haven't seen you around before."

"Yeah." Gus nodded. "I just moved from Minnesota."

"So you can *make* a skateboard, but you can't skate?" Bridger smiled.

"Making it was the easy part," Gus said softly.

There was a pause. Bridger's face lit up with an idea.

"Tell you what. Be here tomorrow, and I'll teach you a thing or two," he offered. "But then? You gotta show me how you made this." Bridger tapped the grip tape of Gus's homemade board as he handed it back to him.

Gus stared down at the concrete and said nothing. Bridger stepped onto his own board and started to ride away. He looked back one last time, facing Gus.

"Tomorrow!" Bridger called out, pointing at him.

"I—okay. Sure, yes! Thank you!" Gus yelled back awkwardly. "I—nice to meet you!"

Bridger continued to skate off into the darkness, leaving Gus standing alone, stunned.

"*Nice to meet you?*" Gus muttered at himself under his breath. *I'm an idiot.*

The next afternoon, Gus showed up well before Bridger did. He decided to practice solo on the patchy road off to the side of the skatepark, not wanting to be near the other local skaters alone. After an hour or so of lousy wobbling and almost-falls, Bridger finally pulled up behind him as Gus almost slipped again.

"Yo, man," Bridger laughed casually, "let's not mess up this early."

Bridger offered Gus a fist bump as he turned around. Gus returned it.

"Check it. Bend your knees a little more." Bridger demonstrated. "Like this."

Bridger showed Gus how to properly balance on his own board. Gus observed every small action as if looking through a microscope.

He stepped back onto his own board, mimicking Bridger's stance.

"Got it," Gus replied. "Like this?"

"Perfect," Bridger confirmed. "Follow me to this flat area here."

Gus got off his board, leaned down, and picked it up with both hands.

"Dude, no," Bridger scoffed. "Don't do that. That's lame. Put it back down."

Gus dropped his board back onto the rough pavement.

"Never bend all the way down to grab your board," Bridger warned. "Pop or kick it up."

Bridger gestured to his own skateboard. He set his foot down on the tail so the board lifted into reach, then grabbed the nose. Gus did the same.

"Great. See? Do that." Bridger let his board fall again. "Or just pop it."

Bridger demonstrated the same movement, only this time he kicked down hard on the tail, making the entire board jump up for him to catch in his outstretched hand.

Gus nodded. After a few failed snags, Gus did the pop successfully. Bridger offered him another fist bump.

"Are you regular or goofy?" Bridger asked.

"Huh?" Gus furrowed his brow.

"Regular is left foot forward, goofy is with your right in front, dummy."

Gus stepped onto his board and glanced at his feet, then stepped off to switch directions. A beat passed before he switched back. "This feels good."

"You're regular. Okay, now use your right foot to pump."

Gus placed his foot down and started pushing, gradually building speed. He was getting the hang of it.

"There you—"

Gus lost control and crashed hard, tumbling off the board. He landed flat on his back in the grassy ditch next to the side road.

"Oh, shit," Bridger muttered, skating over to him.

Soon they moved from balancing and pickups to actual movement. Gus was grateful they were on the side of the park and not in the mix with all the other riders. With Bridger watching, Gus set his foot down to push off and pulled it back onto the board as he wobbled down the pavement. Every bit of his body seemed to shake as the board vibrated across the asphalt.

"How do you stop?!" Gus shouted back.

"Lean on the tail!" Bridger called out.

"The what?"

"The back! Just put your foot down!"

Gus bailed instead, jumping off to the side of the board as it rolled toward the fence. Bridger chuckled as he ran to catch it for him. Once again, Bridger went into demonstration mode, showing Gus how to turn and stop by leaning on the tail of his own board or dragging his shoe.

"You just gotta be less tight. Chill a bit." Bridger smiled.

How he was supposed to chill, Gus didn't know.

For the rest of the day, Gus went back and forth on the same side road as Bridger encouraged him toward steadier balance and smoother stops. He showed Gus some fun ollies and kickflips for inspiration. Eventually, the sun began to set. Gus was getting tired and Bridger was getting hungry.

"I'm starving, dude. I gotta get dinner back at home." Bridger dapped Gus goodbye. "Let's do more tomorrow."

Gus and Bridger both arrived at the park around the same time the next afternoon. Gus was amped to practice but still wanted to use the worn-out side road away from the main concrete. When Bridger's other skater friends arrived an hour later, they all clocked him and Gus from a distance with curious looks. Max squinted with extra suspicion to see Bridger hanging out with the weird kid from his skate shop. Gus tried to avoid their glances, to not think about their judgment. Luckily, Bridger didn't notice their nosy glares. He focused only on Gus.

After practicing more of his basic skills like rolling, stopping, and pickups, Gus began to feel comfortable skating on level surfaces. Bridger knew it was time to show Gus some simple flatground maneuvers like tic-tacs, shuvits, and hippie jumps. Gus was amazed that even the smallest of moves took so much focus and precision. Just lifting his feet off the board for a simple board spin or hop felt impossible. With Bridger's direction and hours of practice, Gus finally landed his first small hippie jump without bailing.

"Good! That took me a week to learn," Bridger congratulated.

"Yeah?" Gus responded with a smile. "I guess I am a quick learner."

Most of the other skaters left for the day, and Bridger and Gus remained. With Bridger's crew gone, Gus finally felt comfortable entering the main concrete of the skatepark. After getting Gus used to the smoother terrain, Bridger tasked him with the exercise of rolling around a bowl. Gus pushed off from the flat center toward the curved bottom and slowly rode up the base of the incline. But, of course, he stepped off before he could roll back down.

"Close!" Bridger encouraged. He skated around the same bowl, adding a tail stall on the rim before rolling back to Gus.

"Do what feels natural. Trust yourself," Bridger explained. "Feel the board beneath your feet."

Next, the boys stood together, both looking ahead at McNair's simple but long pump track. Bridger wanted Gus to skate all the way from the north end of the park to the very south end over all the small bumps and dips. Gus tapped his board nervously against his knee.

"I don't know about this..." Gus warned.

"Don't think, just do it," Bridger pushed.

Gus dropped his board and kicked off, and Bridger watched him go. Gus called up his balance practice, kept his body loose, and just let the wind and shifting forces move his body to the curve of the concrete beneath him. He could feel every slope of the ground underfoot as if his board was now the concrete itself. He was a little wobbly, but before he knew it, Gus had reached the end of the park's smooth mounds and slopes without falling, tail scraping to an awkward stop. He stepped off, kicked up his board, and caught it in his hands. Beaming, he exhaled out all his pent-up anxiety. Gus turned around with a smile to find Bridger proudly clapping back at the opposite side of the skatepark. Both boys were elated.

"Let's go!" Bridger cheered, pumping his fists.

Chapter 4

Secret Bucket

Gus opened the door of his dad's woodshop and let Bridger pass through. He smelled Axe body spray and fresh laundry as the skater boy crossed the threshold of *his* domain for the first time. Gus had been wanting to bring Bridger here for the past few days but had only just felt comfortable inviting him last night.

Gus closed the door behind them. They kept the bright overhead lights off, but plenty of afternoon sun lit the room through the hazy paneled windows. Bridger's scanning gaze soaked in all the scattered lumber and sharp machines in the woodshop. Gus realized he had never been in a room alone with another boy like this before. It felt more personal here than when they skated together at the park with so many others around. Each small step of their feet echoed in the tall, wide space. The sawdust-saturated air felt heavier. Every choice had more weight.

While Bridger touched every single tool and gadget they walked by, Gus gave a free quick tour of the shop. Bridger nodded along while listening.

"—and then after the glued scraps dried," Gus continued explaining, stopping at his own workbench near the window, "I cut out the shape, sanded it, and painted the board right here."

Bridger leaned over to inspect the bandsaw closer. "Shit. You make it sound so easy. I couldn't do any of that."

"Not yet." Gus smiled. "I'll teach you. Just like you're teaching me."

Bridger glanced up from the rotary sander he was tempted to pick up and caught eyes with Gus. He bobbed his head with gratitude and lifted a fist for Gus to bump, holding the new skater's gaze and raising a confident eyebrow.

Each time Bridger smirked at him like this, Gus noticed it. He loved the way it felt. Like they had their own inside joke.

"Your board's going to be awesome," Gus assured.

"Hell yeah!" Bridger hooted. "When can we get started?"

"Actually, I—"

The heavy woodshop door creaked open as Dan stepped into the room from outside. He was carrying a large stack of lumber that covered his face from view. Gus immediately stopped talking, hastily tucked his homemade board under the bench, and stood up straight. He thought his dad would be out at the store longer. Bridger's brow furrowed in confusion at Gus's awkward reaction to seeing his own father.

Dan absentmindedly dropped the new wood planks for the next week's projects onto the main bench, turned around, and finally registered the boys near the woodshop windows. He startled.

"Gus? You're not working today..."

"Uh. Right, I know. Sorry," Gus mumbled, shrinking back.

Dan's eyes darted to Bridger with a quizzical look. "Who's this?"

Bridger adjusted his hair, flashed a big grin, and reached out his palm to Dan. "Nice to meet you, sir."

"This is Bridger," Gus gestured awkwardly.

Dan grunted, surveying all of his nearby equipment as if he knew Bridger had already messed something up with his greasy digits. Regardless, he still extended a reluctant handshake to the boy.

"What're you both doing here?" Dan inquired.

"I'm just showing him around," Gus explained. "How we make all the furniture pieces."

Bridger looked over to Gus with a subtle, unsure squint.

"No using the machines if I'm not around," Dan warned both boys before gesturing to the wood he brought in. "We'll start on the birch first thing Monday. I'll be inside starting dinner. Don't make a mess."

Gus nodded as his father turned around and dropped his work gloves onto a shelf. He walked out of the shed and closed the door. The heavy metal latch shut with a sharp *snap* that rang loudly in the now silent shop.

Bridger twisted toward Gus and peered at him with curiosity. "He doesn't know about your skateboard?"

Gus quickly grabbed his board and pulled Bridger away from the window as Dan strolled past it up to the cabin. He led Bridger to the back of the woodshop. They stood by Gus's secret closet.

"He will, eventually," Gus shared. "I just don't know how he'll react."

"Why? It's cool." Bridger shrugged.

"He doesn't really like... fun?" Gus confided. "He only works. All the time."

"Got it. My parents are the same way. Secret's safe with me," Bridger promised.

Gus opened the door to the storage closet beside them, allowing Bridger to see his contraband. The bucket of leftover wood, half-used glue, expired cans of wood stain, old grip tape, and his skateboard mold were all nestled inconspicuously in the back corner. Bridger's eyes scanned the hodgepodge of materials, bemused that Gus could somehow turn this pile of recycling into a real skateboard.

"I also don't really want him to know I swiped these supplies," Gus admitted.

Bridger lightly toed Gus's secret bucket, jostling its mismatched assortment of lumber. "It's all just scraps. Why would he care?"

"You don't know my dad." Gus placed his skateboard down in the closet next to the wood bucket and covered his board's beautiful mountain design with the crusty, dirty tarp. "Better he knows nothing."

Bridger scoffed. "You guys don't talk much, huh?"

"Not really."

"Well, what about your mom?"

Gus stopped in his tracks. The casual nature of the quick question caught him off guard, and a tidal wave of memories flooded his brain. He hesitated for a moment, staring blankly into the dusty closet as he tried to wade past the emotions to get back to the present moment. Bridger looked up at Gus's eyes in the prolonged quiet, sensing that Gus was seeing something that he never could.

"Uh... she died. Earlier this year." Gus braced for the usual awkwardness. "That's why I moved back with my dad. Way out here."

"Oh," Bridger responded softly.

"Yeah."

Gus closed the closet and walked back to the main portion of the woodshop. Bridger followed, watching his friend intently.

"We're not close. Me and my dad," Gus shared, not looking back. "I lived with my mom, just the two of us, ever since I was five. Pretty soon, I'll leave for college. I'm not here for long."

Gus hadn't had this conversation with anyone in Montana yet. He still didn't know how to handle it. Bridger stepped up next to Gus, back into the window's fresh light.

"Sorry, man. But... glad you're here now," Bridger offered sympathetically.

Gus smiled as he looked up at Bridger. He was relieved when Bridger didn't ask any more questions and just let things be. Bridger simply offered Gus a fist bump with a somber nod of empathy. Gus was grateful. That's all they needed to say.

Needing to cut the tension, Bridger leaned over and reached out with a curious expression to touch a drill press nearby. "So how does this work? Is it used for—"

The drill bit fell out immediately with a loud *clank*. The boys jumped in shock and rushed to put the piece back in place, hoping Dan hadn't heard them.

When stillness returned to the room and Dan didn't show, Gus let a deep breath pass through him. Together, he and Bridger chuckled alone in the shop.

The next morning, Bridger Owens eagerly dashed down his stairs and jumped onto the carpet of his family's living room. He ran for the kitchen, accidentally dropping his board and causing a ruckus as he passed the entryway table adorned with multiple posed family portraits.

Once he'd picked up his board and sped into the busy kitchen, he found his whole family staring at him in alarm. His mother, wearing a purple blouse with her hair tied up in a fraying top bun, poured cereal into bowls. She handed the cereal to Bridger's little sisters, Chloe, Abby, and Cullen, followed by glasses of orange juice. Bridger stomped around as he grabbed his backpack and searched for his shoes. His father was taking notes intently, a phone gluing his ear and shoulder together. He scowled toward Bridger and held his palm up, displeased with all the noise. Bridger didn't notice.

"Bridger, keep it down," Bridger's mom whispered angrily. "Dad's on a work call."

Bridger rolled his eyes as he placed his board in his lap and started lacing his sneakers. "When's he not on a work call?"

"Do you want some breakfast?" his mom asked, irritated.

"Nah. I'm off."

"To the library? Your summer school homework isn't going to finish itself. You can't repeat senior year too, Bridger," his mom reminded intently.

"Yup. Definitely. The library," Bridger affirmed as he headed back through the entryway.

Pulling their house door shut with an echoing *clunk* once he was outside, Bridger dropped his board to the ground and breathed in the fresh air of freedom. He smirked as he kicked off down his suburban street.

"*Sike!*" he exclaimed.

Gus saw Bridger arrive at the skatepark and caught himself smiling as Bridger casually popped onto the concrete with a kickflip. This late June morning was fresh and dewy. They had the park to themselves for now.

"Are you sure you don't want to just skate with your crew when they get here?" Gus asked. "We don't have to practice just 'cause it's my day off."

"Nah. Max is at work for a while." Bridger glanced around. "Most of the guys don't show up until he does."

"Ah, got it."

"It's just you and me." Bridger smirked. "Today, we're doing ollies."

After some minutes of demonstration and Gus scanning Bridger's movements like a fax machine, Gus made some attempts at his first ollies. He failed every time. It was just a simple jumping move, but Gus couldn't nail the carefree balance needed. Gus inhaled and shot forward on his next go, trying to generate momentum. He leaned back to prepare, wobbled, and lost his board as he tried jumping up.

"What are you scared of?" Bridger pressed as Gus's empty board shot past him.

"Falling!" Gus called back. "Duh!"

"It's gonna happen, Gus." Bridger laughed. "Get used to that fear. Just keep your arms tight, tuck, and roll. I'm here for you."

Gus kicked off again and smoothly sped down the concrete slope toward the flat run. He leaned back on his right foot and, without overthinking it, jumped as high as he could into the air. It was only about one actual inch in height, but when his board stayed glued to his feet and followed his small arch, and he landed back on the ground smoothly, a smile burst across his face.

He leveled out and continued speeding down the concrete. "I did it!" Gus beamed, looking back over at Bridger.

"Wait! Watch out!" Bridger dashed toward Gus, seeing the low rail coming into his path.

Gus gasped, swerved, and slammed directly into Bridger.

"Oh, fuck!" Bridger yelped as they both crashed to the ground. Gus's board juddered away as he landed on top of Bridger on the concrete. Both boys grunted in pain.

"Bridger, I'm *so* sorry," Gus lamented, shifting sideways. "Are you okay?"

Yet when Bridger rolled onto his back, Gus saw that he was laughing. Bridger took a deep, long breath, lying flat on the concrete. Gus joined him in turning over.

"*Now* we're skating!" Bridger declared, placing his arms behind his head. He tilted his chin toward Gus to flash a proud smile. "Let's try it again."

Bridger wiped the grit off his scraped knees, popped up, and lent a hand to Gus.

Gus laughed. "Never fazed." He accepted Bridger's helpful reach. "I don't know how you do it."

"'Cause it's fun." Bridger pulled him up.

As Gus stood tall again, he put a foot back on his board. Ready to start another ollie, Gus noticed Bridger was still holding his hand. Bridger then placed his second hand on his shoulder. An electric chill dashed up Gus's spine.

"You've got it. Try again," Bridger encouraged, staring deep into Gus's gaze. He smirked, raising an eyebrow. "Just don't look back at me this time." With a soft chuckle at Gus's startled face, Bridger released his hand.

Gus rolled his eyes at Bridger's mischievous laughter and pushed off to try the ollie again.

Soon other young neighborhood kids started to arrive at the park with their mini helmets and knee pads. Even with them nearby, it took only a few successful ollies and fewer falls for Gus to gain confidence in the move though he was still barely catching air. Bridger eventually asked Gus to connect tricks from previous practice days together, a feat he surprised himself by managing.

Gus was amazed at how much he had learned in only a week. Bridger must have noticed it, too.

"So why'd you wanna learn to skate so bad?" Bridger asked as they took a moment to pause, relax, and sit on the edge of the bowl.

Gus struggled to find a real reason. Truth was, he didn't even understand why.

"I don't know. There's not much to do around here," Gus

decided to say. "Dad has me working all the time. I wanted to try something different."

"Yeah. Skating really is the only shit worth doing in town," Bridger agreed, taking a long, strained breath as he looked around. "I love Livingston, but even *I* get bored here."

Gus squinted at Bridger. Even now, he couldn't picture Bridger as someone who could *ever* be bored. He studied Bridger's face as the boy turned to watch all the other kids on the concrete slopes, catching the corners of his lips quirk up when the kids cackled after they fell down. Gus wondered if Bridger hoped for something different too someday. He wanted to find out.

"Damn, I'm hungry." Bridger whipped his head back toward Gus with a flashy grin. "You want a snack?"

Gus and Bridger skated to the collection of small stores that stood near the skatepark. The excitement of this departure overwhelmed Gus. It felt like he was skipping school for the first time. They spontaneously strolled the Livingston sidewalks, peering into shop windows with their boards under their arms. They passed some quaint cafés and one coffee shop that Gus knew his mom would have loved. But Bridger was craving some candy and beef jerky, so they stopped at a place called *TJ's Gas N Convenience.*

Gus and Bridger entered the shop and perused the skinny aisles. Bridger beelined it to the junk food and pulled out some jerky, a Twinkie, and an orange Fanta. Gus passed the magazine rack and spotted an issue of *Thrasher*. He slipped it free of the metal shelf and flipped through the pages of skateboarders, industry news, and advertisements. While Bridger searched for the perfect bag of chips, Gus placed the magazine, a premade sandwich, a Coke, and some change on the shop counter. He stepped outside to read some of the magazine, sipping his soda while he waited for Bridger.

"Hey! It's Art Boy!" a voice called out.

Gus twisted toward it. The skater girl Gus talked to at the park a few days ago—Tara, if he remembered right—cocked her chin at him with a smile. She walked up to Gus, her skateboard hugged to her side by the crook of her arm. She was wearing a beanie, a baggy graphic tee, ripped jean shorts, and sneakers, looking much cooler than Gus would ever be. In the distance behind Tara, her two other friends walked into a coffee shop.

"How's skating coming along?" Tara inquired.

"Oh. Good," Gus replied, leaning his head toward Bridger in the shop. "Bridger's been teaching me."

"Really? *Bridger* is?"

"Yeah." Gus paused. "Why?"

"I never thought he'd do that," Tara remarked, putting her hand on her hip. "He's usually a dick like the rest of them."

Gus shrugged. "He's fine around me."

Tara appraised Gus. She lifted an eyebrow in thought.

"Maybe because you're nice," she said.

"I'm... nice?" Gus responded, confused.

"Yeah." Tara nodded. "Bridger's not used to that."

A calm pause stalled the conversation. Tara heard the *cha-ching* of the cash register and saw Bridger checking out. Her lips curled into a smile as she thought to herself for a moment before looking back to Gus.

"Catch ya later," Tara remarked slyly as she gave Gus a weird, knowing look.

What's that mean? Gus fretted as Tara rotated away to walk down the street and meet up with her friends at the coffee shop. Gus almost waved as she looked back at him but stopped himself. He didn't know why; he wanted Tara to like him, she was so cool.

Just as Gus took a big bite of his sandwich, Bridger stepped out of the convenience store with a bag overflowing with snacks.

"Bro, check this out," Bridger said, grabbing Gus's arm firmly and yanking him to the side, sending some of the shredded lettuce from his sandwich scattering. Bridger pulled his shorts waistband down, revealing his underwear.

"What the—" Gus almost looked away from the indecent move, but then he saw the imprint of a bottle. The bulge was clearly noticeable behind Bridger's stretched cartoon briefs. Gus gulped. Bridger had a happy trail of soft brown hair that led down from his abs and disappeared beneath his swollen underwear.

Woah... Gus thought. *I don't have that.*

Bridger reached into his briefs, pulling the bottle halfway out to brandish it for Gus. It was a Rainer.

"You're gonna get caught," Gus warned, looking around.

Bridger let go of Gus's arm and donned a devious grin. "Not if we ditch!" he exclaimed, and he immediately bolted down the street.

Gus gasped with worry and followed in a dash behind Bridger. Both boys heaved with exertion until they had safely gotten a few blocks away from the main shops. As they finally slowed, Bridger chuckled at his own shenanigans. Gus laughed along, but his mind drifted elsewhere. He couldn't get the image of the beer bottle in Bridger's underwear out of his head. He looked down at Bridger's hand swaying by his own. He wished Bridger would grab his arm again. The rush of adrenaline had Gus lightheaded.

Gus wondered how Bridger could so eagerly share naughty adventures with him. No other person had ever acted this way around him. Gus didn't know why it felt so strange. All he knew was that he liked it.

"I'll save the prize for after we practice some more tricks," Bridger called back to Gus with a smirk as he skipped a few paces ahead, dropped his board, and hopped on. Within seconds, he was already far down the sidewalk heading back toward the skatepark.

Gus felt nervous for some reason. *Is he always this wild?* In any case, he couldn't help but smile as he watched Bridger ollie off the curb into the street and speed down the road. Snapping out of his mind, Gus jumped on his own skateboard and hurried to catch up.

Chapter 5

Pepper Ketchup & Ice Cream

After a particularly busy Friday working in the woodshop, Gus slept through his alarm the next morning when he was supposed to meet Bridger at the skatepark. When Gus did arrive, lots of other neighborhood kids had already shown up. Bridger was skating by himself.

"Sorry I'm late," Gus huffed as he jogged up.

"It's fine, dude." Bridger smiled. "Let's get at it!"

Bridger wasted no time demonstrating a kickflip to Gus as an advanced flatground trick to try. Gus attempted it a few times but kept losing the board in the air after popping it off the ground. Trying to jump, kick, and land on the narrow board with his balance intact started to seem more a mental feat than a physical challenge by his tenth screw-up. He was losing confidence quickly.

Bridger came over and adjusted Gus's stance and foot position, stepping in close behind Gus's back. Very close.

"One more time," Bridger breathed quietly near Gus's ear. "I know you have it."

Gus's face blushed before he could do anything about it. Luckily, his friend didn't see anything. Bridger stepped away as Gus readied himself for the kickflip. He focused only on the concrete before him.

"Bridger! Where the hell you been?" a voice bellowed out. "You gonna skate with us or what?"

Gus and Bridger turned to see Max, along with Bridger's whole skate crew, arriving at the other end of the park. Boards in hand, the boys eyed Bridger and Gus with confused curiosity.

"Yeah. Hang on!" Bridger called back.

Gus's shoulders dropped as he watched Bridger pick up his board, so quick to leave their practice session.

If Bridger noticed Gus's shift in demeanor, he didn't show it—he was still all smiles. "C'mon. Wanna meet my crew?"

Gus glanced at the other boys. They all stared him down like he was a loose fifth wheel on their boards. Gus breathed in and shook his head.

"Oh, uh. Not yet. I'll just practice solo. I'm not good at making new friends," Gus admitted.

"You sure?"

"Yeah."

"Maybe next time?" Bridger suggested.

Gus looked down at his feet, unsure what to say.

Bridger finally caught on that Gus's energy seemed off, but didn't pry further. Instead he asked, "Wanna go get lunch later? I can meet you at Mark's?"

"Oh. Okay. Yeah! Sure!" Gus said, brightening instantly with surprise.

Bridger's face also lit up as he hopped onto his board.

"Great. Smell ya later," he joked as he pushed off across the waxy concrete to go skate with his other friends.

Gus's grin faded as he watched Bridger go. He was alone again. He looked out to where Bridger and his crew convened. They dapped and cracked jokes and nailed tricks he couldn't remotely understand.

A little girl no more than nine years old sporting oversized knee pads and a loose helmet zoomed past Gus and up the side of the bowl. She aired out, landed on the flat ledge at the other end, and finished with a kickflip. Even she was better at skating than him. Gus felt the sudden, burning urge to run back to his car and drive home. But he was tired of that feeling, tired of being afraid.

He was determined to stay and skate like everyone else.

As Gus turned to face the bowl again, he remembered Bridger's lessons. Stay loose, accept any danger, adjust to whatever sensations happened beneath his feet. Gus gritted his teeth as he pushed off. He shot forward, rolling down the small slope in front of him. When the ground leveled out, he jumped up while kicking the tail of his board behind him so it did a 180 under his feet. He landed back on the board with a shaky finish, but he had finally completed a pop shuvit.

"*Yes!*" Gus exclaimed under his breath, glancing around excitedly, wondering if anyone caught him ace the landing. Maybe Bridger had seen it.

But he hadn't. No one had. Other kids just zoomed around Gus, ignoring him. To them, his big move was nothing special.

Gus peered over at the group of older skate guys at the edge of the park. Bridger was laughing and goofing off with them all. Gus watched them and kicked up his board, trying to muster some confidence.

I can just walk over there. Bridger said I could. He invited me.

Digging his fingernails into his homemade board, Gus took a few steps forward. But, almost as if sensing Gus's intentions, Max glanced over from his skate posse and glared right at him. Gus quickly averted his gaze and stopped walking. With a prolonged sigh, he turned to leave, hurrying back to his car where the comfort of his sketchbook waited.

Afternoon finally hit, and Gus drove to Mark's In & Out a few blocks away. A bright orange neon sign spelled out BEEFBURG-ERS in big bubble letters above the restaurant window. It always reminded Gus of diners from the old artsy films he used to watch with his mom during late Sunday nights, cuddled up under blankets while sipping hot cocoa. The diner itself had this weirdly abstract shape, and as Gus walked up to it, he realized he had never drawn it before. So, sketchbook in hand and backpack slung over one shoulder, he found a vacant red picnic table in the tiny diner's parking lot, took a seat, and pulled out a charcoal pencil.

He had a rough, half-finished sketch of the building by the time he saw Bridger skating up the road. Gus closed his sketchbook hurriedly and stuffed it into his backpack as Bridger kicked up his board and jogged over.

"I know. I'm late," Bridger apologized as he leaned his board up against the table's edge where red paint chips were peeling away from the wood.

"No, not at all." Gus smiled. "Let's eat."

Gus and Bridger went to order food from the diner's front window. Their orders came quickly, and the boys sat down across from each other and wasted no time diving in. Juice dripped down Bridger's hand as he took huge bites of his Pizza Burger while Gus sipped politely from his cream soda. Gus brought up his successful pop shuvit off the bank from that morning, and Bridger hyped him up with proud glee, demanding to see the move next time they practiced while marinara leaked from his lips. He didn't even bother cleaning his mouth until Gus pointed out the smudge of red on his lips. Bridger laughed, stuck out his tongue, and licked the sauce away. Gus had to admire him—the boy never lost his smile, even if things got messy.

Bridger had scarfed his french fries but was now squeezing ketchup packet after ketchup packet onto a paper plate. He added way too many forceful shakes of black pepper on top of the red mound to the point that there was almost more pepper than there was ketchup. Bridger stole one of Gus's fries and dipped it into the concoction.

"Hey!" Gus laughed.

"What? I'm out... and you're too slow," Bridger retorted, inhaling the fry.

"That's a lot of pepper," Gus commented.

"Yeah, it's dank. There's never too much," Bridger said, stealing another fry from Gus, dipping it into the pepper ketchup, and offering it across the table with an assured grin. "Just try it."

"No way!"

"Gus." Bridger nudged it closer and closer to Gus's mouth. "Try it!"

Gus snatched the fry and rolled his eyes. Bridger laughed.

There was so much black pepper on the end of the fry that the ketchup was gray. Begrudgingly, Gus bit into the concoction, fighting off a grimace as it hit his tongue.

Ugh! Way too much.

"It's actually good," Gus lied with a smiling shrug.

Bridger nodded with pride. "Hell yeah, it is!"

He turned around to look back up at the menu board, debating if he needed to order seconds. Gus quickly spat out the pepper-coated fry into a napkin and hid it under the table, shuddering. Bridger turned back to look at Gus.

"I knew you'd like it," Bridger said with a wink.

A wink? Why'd he do that?

As the pair shared his remaining fries, Gus now found himself peeking for too long at Bridger's deep brown eyes, sharp dimples, swooping hair, and constantly moving lips. He liked the shape of all of Bridger's features. He'd be perfect for sketching. Gus watched Bridger's face tilt on an angle, lost in the sight of him as he peered to Gus's left.

"What's that?" Bridger asked, pointing to the sketchbook sitting in Gus's open backpack.

"What?" Gus hesitated. "Oh. Nothing."

Bridger stood up, leaned over, and grabbed the book out of the open zipper before Gus could close it.

"No! Hey!" Gus protested. "It's just drawing practice for school. I didn't say you could—"

As Gus reached to take back the journal, Bridger blocked his hands playfully and opened it.

"Let me look. You can trust me," Bridger said, laughing.

Gus sighed, stopped resisting, and sat back down. He couldn't help but lean over the table awkwardly as Bridger opened the artbook, anxious about his personal drawings being observed. Bridger thumbed through the pages, amazed by all the unfamiliar Minnesota nature scenes and the random people in Gus's ongoing sketches from the months before this summer. Soon, Bridger found the familiar branches of Montana trees and the unmistakable mountains that rose above his small town as he reached Gus's more recent sketches. He nodded his head, awestruck.

"Damn! These are incredible," Bridger exclaimed. "No wonder you got into that fancy art school."

"Um. I'm not that great. I've seen work by their graduates. It's way better than what I do," Gus said modestly.

"Not for long. These pages just keep getting better and better," Bridger remarked.

Bridger flipped the book to a clean page and placed it down in front of Gus. He swiped a pack of colored pencils peeking out from Gus's backpack and handed all the vibrantly shaded tools to him.

"Draw me!" Bridger smirked, tapping the new sheet of paper. "Make it good."

Bridger jokingly struck a stance with his skateboard behind his head as if vogueing for the cover of *Thrasher* or something. He then twisted into a Herculean pose, arms curled like a bodybuilder's.

"Stop it," Gus laughed, throwing a french fry at Bridger.

"I need ice cream," Bridger said, chuckling as he lowered his arms.

Gus guarded their boards as Bridger left to get them both dessert at the counter. He watched Bridger waiting in line. Even just standing there doing nothing, Bridger was effortlessly attractive. Gus picked up a colored pencil, tracing the curve of his sharp jawline, thick eyebrows, and disheveled but stylish hair, and gradually a sketch of Bridger took shape on the page. Gus turned his focus to the ripped-off sleeves of Bridger's T-shirt, the armholes of the deep red material gaping to reveal a toned tan torso underneath. His chest still gleamed with sweat from skating to the diner. It trickled down to where Gus knew that brown hair lay, a fuzzy path that disappeared below his waistband. Gus's grip on his pencil loosened.

"Found your muse, Art Boy?"

Gus jumped. He turned to see Tara standing behind him holding some chili cheese fries. This time, instead of the skater gear he was used to her wearing, she had her braided hair down and wore a checkered denim skirt and cropped lilac tee. She held a journal and a pen under her fries.

Tara nodded over to Bridger in the ice cream line. "Looks like you two are becoming friends after all."

"Oh. I don't know if he's my actual friend," Gus deflected. "We just have this deal where—"

Tara chuckled wistfully to interrupt him and gestured to Bridger at the cashier.

"If he's getting you ice cream, and you're drawing him..." Tara trailed off, glancing down at Gus's sketch. He tried to cover the drawing. Tara raised her eyebrow and gave him a smirk. "...then he's, at the bare minimum, your friend," Tara finished. "Let me see."

Gus relented and Tara leaned over to view the simple sketch.

"We were just skating," Gus replied, "and came here because we're hungry."

"Seems like it," Tara quipped, flashing a teasing smile.

Gus shrunk in perplexed embarrassment, not knowing what to say in response. At the same time, Bridger turned to look from the cash register toward their table and spotted Gus with Tara. His face lifted with sly shock and pride as he paused in the distance to watch without interrupting.

"We haven't said we're friends yet," Gus admitted awkwardly.

Tara hopped onto the table. "You don't have to ask someone to be your friend. You just feel it." She smiled. "I'm Tara, by the way."

"I'm Gus... are you writing something?" he asked, indicating the journal in Tara's arms.

"These are my notes."

"For what?"

"I have a job interview tonight," Tara explained. "Trying to make use of my computer science degree somehow."

"That's cool! I'm going to art school in Rhode Island this fall," Gus shared.

"Art college? Good!" Tara said. "Glad you won't be stuck in this podunk town like everyone else."

"It's not that bad here," Gus defended with a grin.

"Easy for you, white boy. I'm the only Black girl for miles," Tara joked.

Gus realized Tara was the only other person in town beyond Bridger who wanted to talk with him. She was so bold and interesting, unlike Gus himself. He wished he could be like her, have the same confidence she did. *So why me? Why is she talking to me?*

"I just need something new." Tara breathed in slowly. She looked up and shook her head, seemingly lost in thought. Gus watched as she seemed to exhale years of tension. "I figure, maybe a coding job in California can get me out of here," she said. "Plus, the skate scene in LA is way better."

They both laughed, sharing smiles like old friends.

"I've never been to a big city like that," Gus remarked. "Sounds amazing."

Tara paused and took in Gus. He was so kind and gentle-natured—different from all the other boys in Livingston.

"You will. We both will," Tara said, holding Gus's gaze like a promise.

Back at the counter, Bridger's expression turned to something both unsure and eager as he privately watched Gus with the hot older college girl. He tried to correct his face when he caught Gus looking over.

Tara turned from Gus, following his line of sight to Bridger, now holding two ice cream cones. She smiled somberly as she twisted back to Gus. "Not everyone's like Bridger. People aren't very accepting here." She hesitated. "If you ever need advice... let me know."

Gus tilted his head in curiosity, not sure what she meant. Behind Tara, a car turned on, music blaring from the open windows as it backed up. Inside were a couple of older-looking girls—more of Tara's friends. Some had skateboards, some had books, but all of them had chili cheese fries just like Tara.

"Tara!" one of them blurted out. "We gotta go!"

Tara whipped around and her face lit up.

"One sec!" Tara called out to her friends before beaming back at Gus. "You'll build your own *real* crew one day. Don't settle for anything less. Okay, Gus?"

Gus nodded in acknowledgment but somehow felt like he'd missed something she was trying to tell him.

"See you around. Enjoy your... *friend*," Tara remarked jauntily as she popped a final chili cheese fry into her mouth.

She twisted to leave and hopped into the car with her girls. An Avril Lavigne song faded into the distance as they drove off. Immediately, Bridger rushed up to Gus from the sidelines with the cones.

"Dude! How the hell did you get Tara Shae to talk to you?" Bridger exclaimed.

"I don't know, she came up to me both times," Gus replied.

"Both times?! She talked to you *twice*?"

"Wait, no. Three. I ran into her at TJ's, too."

Bridger coughed with delight, almost dropping the ice cream in his hands. "Gus, Tara's the hottest girl in town *and* she skates! All the guys cream their pants when she walks by."

Gus laughed. "Really?"

"I gotta tell the guys. They're gonna think you're a god!" Bridger boasted.

"She seems to like me and I'm not doing anything." Gus shrugged.

"It's the art—your sketches. You're a total babe magnet," Bridger chided, pushing Gus's head with his forearm.

Gus laughed again as Bridger nodded with satisfaction, pride, and newfound respect.

"How much for the ice cream cone?" Gus asked.

"It's on me, dude. You've earned it," Bridger replied.

Gus closed his sketchbook on the unfinished drawing of Bridger and accepted the congratulatory ice cream cone the skater boy handed him. Bridger sat down on Gus's side of the red wooden picnic table and they enjoyed their desserts together.

That evening, Bridger invited Gus to his favorite lake just outside town to go swimming. As soon as they pulled up to the waterfront, Gus watched as Bridger raced toward the water and confidently ripped off all his clothes down to his underwear. He jumped off the dock and cannonballed into the water, carefree.

Gus delayed joining. He slowly unlaced his shoes and shyly took off his shirt on the dock.

"C'mon!" Bridger called out from the water. "Jump in!"

"Is it cold?" Gus asked nervously as he sat down on the wooden ledge.

"Don't be a pussy! Stop thinking and just have fun!" Bridger reached up and yanked on Gus's arm, dragging him into the lake.

Gus yelped as they both sank underwater. He forced his eyes shut as a frigid wet shock engulfed his entire body. He shot back up to the surface quickly, wiping water out of his eyes.

"Bridger!" Gus yelled, splashing him. Bridger splashed back.

"What? It worked! No more nerves." Bridger floated in closer. "You're here now."

Gus's teeth chattered and Bridger laughed. A double image of both boys reflected in the level surface of the lake as they treaded water. They both broke out into grins.

The boys swam, splashed, and dunked each other in the lake until they'd had their fill and settled on the wooden dock to rest and chat. The world was still and quiet around them as they lay there, spent and shirtless in their wet underwear. The glow of the evening sun cascaded over the mountains onto the lake and warmed their skin. Gus was hyperaware of Bridger's half-naked body beside him. It was so close he could actually touch it. *Don't look down,* Gus told himself.

However, while Bridger told a funny story about the last time he came to this lake with his buddies Coop, Avery, and Bennet, Gus couldn't help but follow the beads of water dripping down his friend's defined stomach. Gus watched each ab flex in turn when Bridger laughed. *Why don't my muscles do that?*

Bridger put his arms behind his head, revealing the small tufts of brown hair beneath them. Gus could literally feel heat radiating off Bridger's body. He had the sudden urge to snuggle in closer. Gus hated that he wanted to scan more of Bridger's strong, tanned, shirt-less body, but he did. He wanted to absorb it, explore it.

It's all right there. Right next to me.

As Gus's eyes slowly drifted toward Bridger's lake-soaked briefs, he caught himself. He snapped his gaze back up and nodded along to Bridger's story even though his attention stayed elsewhere. He couldn't let Bridger catch him ogling.

Why am I such a freak?

Gus forced himself to focus on the purple clouds above and enjoy the sunset's deep golden rays. After Bridger finished his story, the boys shared a few minutes of calm, comfortable silence on the dock. Bridger sighed peacefully. He turned to peer at Gus, eying him up for an extended period of time.

Gus felt Bridger's unabashed gaze on him. *What's he doing now?* He glanced back at Bridger, confused.

"...What?" Gus asked with a soft laugh.

Bridger looked Gus up and down again. "I still can't believe Tara talked to you today," he remarked.

Gus shrugged and stared back up into the tree branches above them.

"You gonna ask her out?" Bridger asked in a more serious tone.

"I don't know. She's not really my type," Gus confessed.

"Not your type?!" Bridger scoffed with a growing smile. "Hot girls aren't Gus's type?"

"Well, yeah. They are." Gus chuckled in nervous defense.

"I'm gonna try to ask out her friend Sophia," Bridger shared, nodding with determination. "All the guys think she's hot, too."

"Yeah?"

"Yeah. If we got with Tara and Sophia, that'd be rad. Who've you hooked up with?" Bridger inquired with a curious glance.

Gus paused and cleared his throat. "This girl... Lauren... back in Minnesota," he lied.

"Daaaaaamn. Okay, Gus! What'd you do?" Bridger pressed with excitement, sitting up.

Gus sat up, too. "Oh, you know. The usual stuff..." he replied evasively.

"Did she...?" Bridger raised his eyebrows suggestively and pushed his tongue into his right cheek to simulate a blow job. Gus nodded, going along with the lie.

"Mmmhmmm. Oh, totally," Gus confirmed.

Bridger smirked slyly. "Did you, you know, finger her?" he whispered.

Gus's eyes widened in shock, surprised by how forward Bridger was being about sex stuff. He didn't know what to say, but he felt excited and intrigued.

"Yes. Yep," Gus replied, continuing the lie.

"Niiiiiice," Bridger affirmed.

Both boys leaned back on the dock. Gus pondered for a moment before looking back at Bridger.

"Okay. Maybe I will ask Tara out," Gus said.

"Yeah you will!" Bridger encouraged, rapping on Gus's chest.

Bridger then pushed Gus into the water and hooted as Gus yelped in fear.

After the two boys had gone home that night, Gus had a late dinner with his father and retired to his bedroom. He finished coloring his drawings from the burger joint at his desk and eventually slunk under his covers. As he dropped his shirt near the wooden trunk next to his bed, it fell on the copy of *Thrasher* he had bought at TJ's. Gus picked it up, realizing he hadn't actually gotten a chance to read it through yet. He flipped on his bedside lamp and thumbed through the magazine.

On the third page, Gus stopped on an over-sexualized gambling advertisement with a scantily clad woman in a casino. The girl was beautiful but clearly had on heavy makeup and lay almost naked with her back arched uncomfortably on a poker table. Big words above her head asked, *WANNA PLAY?*

Gus paused as he looked at the woman. He knew Bridger and his friends would be drooling over this girl. He realized, after a moment, that he should want her as well. But as Gus thought about what this woman must have been asked to do for this picture, he found his nose naturally scrunching up in annoyance and disgust.

He turned the page.

The next spread opened on an image of a shirtless skater flipping in midair at a skatepark. He wore a backward cap and cool sneakers, and a tank top hung from his back pocket. His chest looked strong and sweaty, and finished in a little trail of hair that followed his abs down to under his belt... Gus brought the image closer to his face to examine the guy's happy trail. He paused again, catching himself. This image, he knew he shouldn't like, but he couldn't help staring.

Gus flipped the pages back and forth between both the woman and the man a few times. He forced himself to stay on the picture of the girl. *I can like her better, I know I can.* But no. He couldn't stop himself from flipping the page back to the photo of the man.

He's just another guy. I just want to skate like him. That's it. I don't like him...

Yet Gus breathed in and stared at the skater even deeper. With all the guilt of secret shame, he let his gaze linger and soak up every ripple of the man's body.

He kinda looks like Bridger...

A jolt of humiliation, embarrassment, and sadness overcame him. Gus didn't know why. He laid his head back and closed his eyes. Suddenly, he had to squeeze his face tightly so as not to let tears fall out. Gus slammed the magazine shut and tossed it away.

Chapter 6

Gay or Somethin'

One evening the next weekend, Bridger pulled up to Dan's property in his beat-up blue Chrysler Neon, a hand-me-down that his parents no longer used. Gus met him outside and the pair of boys snuck into Dan's woodshop.

"My dad's in town buying more supplies. Let's be quick," Gus reminded Bridger as he closed the door.

The windows were growing darker. Only small side lamps glowed inside. Gus led Bridger to his secret closet where all the items they needed to build another board were hidden. He grabbed the bucket of wood scraps and lifted it up.

"Ready for a board of your own?" he asked.

"You know it!" Bridger shot back.

Gus took the lead in all the carpentry steps as Bridger tried his best to assist without getting in the way. Over their few short weeks of skateboarding practice, Gus had explained the board-making process to Bridger multiple times. Bridger had thought he understood it, but it was a whole other beast to actually watch it happen before him. He flinched when Gus flipped on the table saw, the screeching buzz so much louder than he'd expected. But as Gus sent the wood scraps through the dangerous machine to thin out, level, and cut each piece evenly, Bridger's alarm softened to contentment. It was easy to adapt when Gus was so calm. Bridger warmed to see this side of Gus. Confident Gus.

The boys arranged the wood scraps together on the main worktable. Gus had Bridger squeeze glue between each piece as he layered them together.

"Shoot, I forgot the clamp." Hands occupied with the huge stack of sticky wood, Gus jutted his chin toward his supplies. "Go get it back there."

Bridger dashed off to the closet and Gus heard loud clanking as Bridger shuffled all the contents around, probably making a mess.

"This long red thing?" Bridger called back. Another *bang* resonated.

"Yes!" Gus answered, still holding the wood pieces tight. "Also, can you be less... loud?"

Bridger returned with the clamp and a smile, and the boys switched positions, Bridger holding the wood strips while Gus secured the clamp and twisted it taut. Together they lifted the layered wood structure off the table and stashed away Bridger's developing board in the same place Gus's once sat.

"Okay. Now it needs a day to dry out," Gus explained as he locked the closet door.

"Dude, that was wicked." Bridger elbowed Gus lightly. "I'm pumped. When do we do the next steps?"

"Maybe... Wednesday night?" Gus suggested. "We just need my dad to be in town or asleep."

"Got it," Bridger confirmed. He paused to look around the empty space. "Does... your dad have any booze?"

"Uh..." Gus mumbled.

Gus took Bridger across the yard and into his family's cabin for the first time. Bridger peered around the peaceful but empty home. The interior was full of homemade wooden furniture, had pine-planked walls, and featured a rugged stone fireplace. Gus watched Bridger nodding to himself as they walked toward the kitchen. The house must have explained a lot about Gus.

In the fridge, they found some leftovers from the dinner Dan had cooked last night and one lone beer in the back. Gus grabbed the bottle and offered it to Bridger.

"You have it," Gus said.

Bridger cracked the lid and took a big glug.

"Good stuff." Bridger sighed with contentment, reveling in the refreshment after all their woodworking. He held the drink out to Gus. "Here, taste it."

Gus accepted the beer with slow hesitation.

"Oh! Going for it?" Bridger quirked a devilish eyebrow. "Didn't know you had a wild side, Gus."

"Me neither," Gus admitted as he swigged from the bottle carefully. The taste was terrible. *Why do people drink this?*

"I like you wild," Bridger replied. "Looks good on you."

Gus smiled. Bridger then rapped the bottom of the beer bottle playfully, and it foamed over.

"Hey!" Gus jumped back in surprise.

Bridger laughed as beer spilled all over the floor.

Outside McNair Skatepark, Bridger and Gus met in the pebbly parking lot and strolled casually toward the concrete. Bridger saw his crew of skater friends, waved, and turned back to Gus.

"Let's skate with them today," Bridger suggested.

"Oh. No. I'm not good enough yet," Gus hesitated.

"It's fiiiine!" Bridger waved his hand. "We all used to be rookies. Come on."

Gus shook his head. "I don't think—"

"Max *can* be harsh. But that's just 'cause he's so fuckin' good."

Bridger kept walking. Gus followed, realizing he had no choice.

Bridger eagerly stepped down into the bowl and approached his closest friends: Avery, Bennet, and Coop. Gus trailed behind. More of Bridger's crew sat on the bowl's other edge intently watching Max skate nearby.

"Aye, Bridge." Avery stood up, noticing Bridger.

"What's good!" Bridger responded with a dap.

Bennet bobbed his head at Bridger as he cracked some peanuts and downed a handful. Coop was lying against a vertical ramp, smoking a joint.

The small group of boys all turned as Max caught massive air off a spine, then landed a heelflip.

"What's he going for?" Bridger asked.

"A tre flip into a backside 180," Avery answered.

Bridger nodded. "Nice." He bumped Gus with his arm. "Also, guys, this is Gus. He's new in town."

Avery, Bennet, and Coop all shifted Gus's way. They smiled absentmindedly and offered him fists to bump. Gus completed the hand gestures with a weak fist but a growing smile, shocked to be included. He held his homemade board behind his back.

Max landed his complex skate line and the boys jolted back around to give him their attention. The whole group tapped their boards on the concrete in a cacophony of approval. Gus stayed silent while Bridger leaned in toward his friends.

"Yeah, I'm teaching Gus how to ride. Pretty soon, he'll be as good as Max." Bridger sent a sly, confident wink Gus's way.

"I doubt that, Bridge," Max interrupted, overhearing them as he skated toward their group.

All the younger boys parted like the Red Sea.

"Why's he here?" Max barked toward Bridger, kicking up his board and ignoring Gus.

"This is Gus. He's got this sweet board—"

"I've seen him around. He's always watching us... like a creep," Max snarled, finally turning to Gus.

Gus's face contorted in stunned embarrassment as Max sized him up.

"Yeah," Max went on. "Same broke ass who came into my shop."

He chuckled at Gus's fright. "And now you follow me here? What...? You gay or somethin'?"

Those words hit Gus like bricks. *Gay?* His stomach flipped. His legs turned to jelly.

"Dude, no way!" Bridger shook the words off like a bad joke. "Gus is cool. Even Tara has the hots for him."

Max's eyebrows pulled into a V. This news had irked him. He turned on both boys viciously. "He can't even skate!"

"He's learning," Bridger interjected, caught off guard. "And—"

"He's just a poser." Max stepped tauntingly toward Gus. "A shrimpy wannabe."

The other skate boys erupted into a collective *Ohhhhh!* at the insult, bringing their fists to their mouths.

Gus didn't know what to say. He looked down. Some of the boys' snickers felt vicious, others were just chuckles of unease... but every mocking stare burned the same. The only person who didn't laugh was Bridger.

Gus wanted to run away, but his feet were too weak to move.

Bridger's chin lifted in slight defiance. "I'm teaching him."

Max twisted back to Bridger forcefully. "Why?! You skate with me."

"I'm—I'm just here to learn," Gus struggled to interject. "Sorry if I did something back at—"

"Whatever," Max interrupted. "Our crew is big enough."

"I, uh..." Gus stuttered.

Bridger grabbed Gus's board from behind his back.

"Look what he can build though!" Bridger exclaimed, lifting it high while Gus still held on to the other side of it. The pair ended up displaying the board between them like a trophy.

A cruel grin spread across Max's face. "What dumpster was that rotting in?" he jeered, turning to the other skaters to encourage their derision as well.

However, as all the young skaters darted in closer to view the board, they lit up, eyes tracing the board's painted mountain design and thicker sturdiness. They all reached out to touch it. Bridger looked to Gus, who gave a small shrug, and let the board leave his hands to sail among the crew's hands.

"Dude! Where did you buy this?" Bennet marveled at Gus.

"He made it himself," Bridger bragged. "I'm actually hoping to—"

"Damn! How do I get one?" Avery jumped in.

"Gnarly, dude!" Coop added.

Max shifted sideways as the rest of the crew pushed past him to feel the board's paintwork. Even the other skaters and local scooter kids nearby glanced their way.

"Guys! Shut it," Max hissed, yanking on the board. "We can't have our crew riding shitty decks."

The boys all let go of Gus's board as Max pulled it away.

"Get your gear from my dad's shop or you're out," Max bellowed. "No one's gonna take you seriously riding this garbage."

The group all went quiet. The mood shifted. No one wanted to get kicked out of Max's skate crew.

Max breathed back in, glad he'd maintained order.

Bridger moved to grab the board back, but Max jerked it out of reach.

"C'mon, Max." Bridger slung his head back in annoyance. "He's getting better."

"Okay. Fine." Max tossed the board to the ground in front of Gus's feet. "Show us a trick."

Gus's heart pounded in his chest. He knew he could *not* land any tricks. Not like this.

Bridger turned to Gus and whispered, "You don't have to."

Gus, petrified, didn't think he could walk, let alone skate.

"Well?" Max taunted, crossing his arms. "Everyone's waiting."

Gus peered around. Indeed, every eye was glued on him. He swallowed hard, his palms leaking sweat, and stepped onto his board.

Max glanced at a nearby skater and whispered something that made the guy snicker.

Gus pushed off, gliding smoothly across the pavement. For a brief moment, he felt steady, but as he crouched to attempt an ollie, his confidence crumbled. The board shot out from under him, and he landed smack on his ass.

Laughter erupted from the crew, loud and relentless. Max's

crude guffaws rang above the others. Only Bridger remained silent.

"Pathetic," Max spat at Gus. He put a foot on his Santa Cruz and glared at Bridger. "You can't make new friends."

Bridger almost laughed. "What?"

"You skate with me. With us. You don't play arts and crafts with... girls," Max declared, throwing a disgusted look at Gus, still on the ground.

Bridger said nothing. The tension was thick as concrete. The group widened, stepping even farther from Gus on the ground.

Max kicked off and skated toward a distant handrail. "Drop him, Bridge," he tossed back as he skated away. "Don't waste your time."

Most of the group immediately followed Max like sheep, leaving Gus and Bridger behind. Coop, Bennet, and Avery gave Gus and Bridger nods or kind waves but left as well.

Bridger turned to a shaken Gus below him and rolled his eyes, pretending to brush off the moment. But deep down, even he was rattled.

"He's just fucking with you. Ignore him," Bridger said. "He's like that to everyone."

Gus didn't respond. He got up, brushed grit from his palms, and picked up his board. Without a word, he started to walk away.

"Gus. Wait." Bridger stepped after him. He grabbed Gus's shoulder, stopping him. "You just gotta practice more," Bridger said softly.

Gus shrugged off Bridger's hand. "It's fine," he replied, curt, and carried on ahead.

"Max will come around. You'll get better, and he'll bring you into the crew. I know it," Bridger assured Gus, trailing after.

"Right. Sure," Gus replied distantly. He knew they were both lying to themselves.

Bridger took a few more steps. "Wanna hang later?"

"I have work to do," Gus said without looking back.

Bridger stopped following and sulked alone on the concrete.

He watched Gus race back to his car.

The next morning, while oiling a new cherrywood coffee table with his dad in the woodshop, Gus's mind drifted to yesterday's utter mess. He feared Bridger might not want to skate with him ever again. They hadn't made plans to skate over the upcoming weekend, so Gus was lost on where they stood. He couldn't blame Bridger if he *did* ditch him. Bridger had known Max and his friends for years and Gus only a few weeks. He was the outlier everyone hated. Somehow he had caused a rift in their crew without meaning to.

What if Bridger fully ignores me next time?

The idea of returning to the park only to be shunned consumed Gus's attention for the rest of his workday.

For dinner, Dan cooked up some seared steak, glazed carrots, and whipped parsnips with an onion gravy. It was a delicious yet quiet meal, like all the others. As he and his father ate in silence, Gus returned to his thoughts. Without the skatepark, he'd have to abide this awkward, lonely stillness every single day. The weight of the remainder of his summer grew heavier.

The *brrring* of their corded wall phone cut through the supper haze. It was a shock to Gus's ear. No one ever called this late.

Gus looked up with confusion at his father. "Another order?"

"Probably," Dan grunted as he stood from his chair to pick up the phone.

After a few seconds of pleasantries, his father raised his eyebrows in surprise.

"It's for you," Dan grumbled casually as he looked over at Gus. "What?"

His dad brandished the phone.

"Oh." *For me?* Gus took the phone from his father's hands with a curious face and put it to his ear.

"Hey, Gus. It's Bridger," the calm voice opened on the other end of the line.

"Oh. Hello," Gus replied as his stomach bottomed out. *This is it. I'm being ditched.*

"Instead of practicing at the skatepark tomorrow, can I come around to yours?" Bridger asked breezily.

Gus's head tilted back in surprise.

"Let's skate on the roads near you. That'll be good to try. Plus, I think the guys aren't *quite* ready for you yet." Bridger chuckled.

"Oh. Uh, yeah. Sure," Gus agreed. He bit a lip in contemplation. *They're never gonna be ready.*

"Great. Can we also finish my board? It's probably dry now, right?" Bridger asked.

Gus's eyes darted to his father at the table. He twisted the phone away to ensure his dad heard nothing.

"Uh, yeah, we can do that," Gus worded carefully. His dad looked up, and Gus put his hand over the phone. "Can Bridger come by tomorrow?"

Dan sighed. "To do what?"

"He wants to… get out of town," Gus lied. "See the woods and trails near us."

"He can visit after we finish the redwood desk order," Dan replied.

Gus lifted the phone back to his ear. "I'll probably finish work around late afternoon. You can come after that."

"Great. Catch you then!" Bridger concluded cheerfully.

Gus hung the phone back up on the wall and sat back down to finish his food.

"Make sure Bridger stays out of the shop this time," Dan said. "We can't afford any injuries."

"Yes, sir," Gus lied again, confirming his father's rule with a deceptive nod.

Dan returned to eating his steak and parsnips. Gus sulked in his chair, his secrets a growing burden. He stared at his plate with guilt.

What am I doing?

The next afternoon, when the bell above the woodshop door chimed, Dan looked up from the desk they were constructing. Gus's eyes widened in surprise as Bridger entered. Gus put down some carpentry tools and pushed forward.

"Bridger! Let's meet outside."

"Oh?" Bridger responded with surprise as Gus led him out. "Okay, dude."

Gus popped his head back in the shop.

"I finished everything on my end. Is it okay if we head out?" Gus asked his father. "I'll clean later."

"Don't be out too late," Dan grunted, brushing off the surface he'd just sanded. "I have to drive into town later."

"I know. You told me." Gus put on a smile. "We'll be back before it's dark."

Dan nodded as Gus left the shop. He watched the boys walk toward his cabin through the window. His head tilted in thought and his gaze narrowed, then he lifted his brows. He didn't understand why he felt almost... worried. Alone again, Dan set to polishing the redwood desk.

After Gus quickly ran upstairs and grabbed his board from its hiding spot in his room, he met Bridger back at his front door and together they walked out to the main road off the gravel driveway. The boys skated down an empty road a ways off from Dan's property, winding back and forth in front of each other. Bridger seemed a little more distant than normal to Gus. He mentioned a few tidbits, like how skating long distances and on hills would be good practice for Gus, but for the most part stayed quiet. Soon, the blue afternoon sky morphed into the golden glow of sunset. As the boys approached a long stretch of smooth paved road with a slight downhill slope, Bridger kicked off the ground a few extra times and sped far out in front of Gus.

"Hey! Slow down!" Gus called out.

Bridger didn't look back. He kept speeding forward.

"NEVER!" Bridger yelled jokingly, lifting his arms like a soaring airplane. He basked in the sunlight and let the wind rush through his hair and run all around his body.

With his eyes closed and arms out wide, surrendering to any danger that might come, Bridger called back, "When I skate really fast, it feels like I'm flying."

"I can't go that fast!" Gus protested, trying to catch up.

"Do it! You forget all the shit you don't wanna think about."

"Or I fall flat on my face!" Gus retorted.

Bridger grumbled dramatically, rolled his eyes, and decelerated to a stop. He turned back to wait for an approaching Gus to come to a sloppy pause at his side. Bridger suppressed a laugh.

"Fine, I'll slow down," Bridger conceded with a smirk. "For *you*."

The boys both kicked off again and continued to ride in tandem. While they cruised side by side, Bridger turned to glance at Gus.

Gus looked back. Bridger seemed apprehensive but eager to mention something.

"Don't tell Max this, but Avery, Bennet, and Coop told me they really like your board. They all want their own," Bridger revealed.

"Oh?" Gus responded.

"They'd even pay for it," Bridger added, sounding smug.

"Really?" *The crew wants my boards?*

"Yeah, and I think the other guys would too if we design cool decks," Bridger continued.

"I don't know. We still haven't finished your board... And we don't have that many extra supplies. Dad might think I'm stealing if we make more decks." Gus hesitated.

"They're scraps! He probably throws that wood in the fire anyway," Bridger reasoned.

Gus breathed in, a bit nervous, but nodded.

The boys continued to skate down the road under the deepening orange of sunset, weaving back and forth. When they arrived back at Dan's property under the evening's violet sky, Gus saw that his father's car was not in the driveway. His dad had left to go pick up their wood order for next week.

"He's gone." Gus nudged Bridger. "Let's do your board now."

Gus led Bridger into the woodshop and they both immediately got to work. Gus unlocked the closet, and together the boys carried the heavy clamped skateboard mold to the main bench. Bridger watched as Gus showed how to cut out the oval deck shape from the dried layered wood with the bandsaw. Next, they had to smooth the edges with a rotary sander. Gus demonstrated how to stand while holding the corded machine to level the board's surface properly.

"It's crazy seeing it in this shape," Bridger called out over the sander. "It's so close!"

Gus pressed the off switch so they could talk. He handed Bridger the sander.

"Here. You try this bit," Gus encouraged. "Sanding is easy."

Bridger laughed. "Dude, no. I'll fuck it up somehow."

"You can do it," Gus comforted. "It's my turn to teach you. It's easier than skateboarding."

Bridger breathed in, then switched on the sander. He started the same actions Gus had shown him, but the power tool shook forcefully and left his movements jittery.

Gus chuckled. He reached out to give Bridger's hands a firmer press so that it put more pressure on the electric sander. Bridger smiled, surprised by the confident, guiding touch. Together, they moved the machine in the proper circular motions. Bridger bobbed his head excitedly with new understanding. The boys linked eyes for a moment as they smoothed out the left edge of the skateboard as a pair. Then Gus dropped his hands to let Bridger keep practicing on his own. It didn't take long before Bridger got the motion down, shifting his weight to finish the right side of the board.

"You're doing great," Gus encouraged.

"It's *so cool* you know to do all this," Bridger replied.

The woodshop door opened with a loud *creak* and Gus's father walked in.

The boys jumped apart quickly, trying to act casual. Dan was taken aback. His eyes darted between both boys.

"You're back!" Gus sputtered.

"What are you two doing?" Dan asked sternly.

"Uh, just practicing what you taught me," Gus replied.

"But I told you, no using the machines without me knowing," Dan reminded him, growing frustrated.

"I mean, by this point, I know how to use them."

"Gus. Don't get smart. I also said not to have Bridger in here."

Bridger glanced over at Gus, looking a bit slighted. Gus had lied to Bridger, too.

Dan looked down and saw the buckets of wood scraps and tools. "Is that wood from my inventory?" he questioned, louder now.

"No. Well, j-just the scraps," Gus stuttered, feeling cornered.

Dan sighed. "We still use those for other projects. No wonder expenses are up."

"Oh. I didn't know—"

"It was my idea," Bridger cut in, protecting Gus.

"What was?" Dan probed.

"Making skateboards."

Dan switched back to his son. "Making... skateboards? Gus, you need to focus on your work. Then college. Not some dangerous hobby," Dan lectured.

Gus exhaled, giving up. "I work all the time now. I saw other guys skating in town and... I really wanted a board, but I couldn't afford it," Gus explained. "So I made one from the extra wood. I'm sorry."

"Skateboarding? But... why? It just... seems like a waste of time." Dan shook his head, confused. "Why didn't you tell me?"

"I don't know," Gus admitted. "I guess I was just embarrassed about it all."

"Sorry, sir. I asked him to build me another one too," Bridger added.

Dan looked between both boys, squinting. He was more annoyed than upset. The boys stayed silent.

"My shop sells furniture. We're not equipped for skateboards," he stated firmly.

Both boys looked down. When he saw the state Gus was in, Dan softened.

"Gus, I'm not angry. I'm just disappointed you kept this from me," Dan said.

"Well, you don't talk to me much either," Gus retorted. "We barely know each other."

Dan's eyebrows raised in affronted surprise and Gus immediately regretted what he'd said.

Bridger looked between them both. Anxious to ease the tension, he pulled out Gus's hidden board from beneath the bench and placed it next to the one they had almost finished for him.

"I think you'd be proud of his work, sir," Bridger stated.

Dan glanced down at the board, still perturbed. However, as he inspected the wooden deck, his grimace of frustration molded into intrigue. He looked up at the boys.

"You did this yourself, Gus?" Dan asked.

"Yeah," Gus replied.

"You should've done your rip cuts on the table saw, but you've certainly improved," Dan said, rubbing the smooth grain. He squinted. "But again, why make boards like this? Why all the extra effort?"

Gus shrugged, letting go. He was finally ready to be honest.

"I'm just... trying to make some friends," Gus admitted.

The shop was silent. Dan stared at his son. He glanced at Bridger, then back at Gus. Then, with a mighty exhale, Dan grabbed a new piece of sandpaper.

"Alright. Move over. Let me help you polish this off better," the seasoned craftsman offered.

"What?" Gus asked.

"You already put all this work in, so you can keep at it," Dan conceded. "Just tell me next time you plan on taking from my supply. Got it?"

"Yes, sir," Gus agreed.

His dad's hands stopped above the board and stilled for a moment. "No more sir. Call me Dad," his father corrected.

Gus paused upon hearing that statement, finally smiling as his dad put paper to board.

In a quick series of movements, Dan smoothed out Bridger's board with ease, wielding the sandpaper like a sculptor. He touched up the board's edges, then walked off to open a fresh jar of sealant. The boys stayed firmly put and watched while he worked. Dan deftly poured the varnish onto Bridger's unpainted deck and wiped away the excess with a beveled scraper.

"Damn! Now mine's smoother than Gus's!" Bridger proclaimed, buzzing with excitement.

"Thanks, Dad," Gus quietly said as he bowed his head slightly, catching his father's eye. "I'll put the wheels on later."

"Will you help us build more decks for my friends?" Bridger asked. "They'll buy 'em!"

Dan chuckled lightly at Bridger's boldness.

"I can show you the process I've done so far," Gus added in.

Seeing his son take initiative, the corners of Dan's mouth twisted upward with a subtle, proud satisfaction. He leaned against the workbench.

"Fine, but not tonight," Dan replied, then turned to their guest. "Bridger, are you spending the night?"

Gus froze. *He can stay over?*

Bridger perked up. "Oh! Sure. I'll stay if I can."

"Great. I'm going to bed. No more secrets, okay?" Dan peered at his son.

Gus turned serious, eyed Bridger, then nodded back to his dad.

"Good. You both clean up here. See you in the morning," Dan said, pulling off his work gloves and walking toward the exit.

Once Dan left the shop, Bridger picked up the new deck. The fresh polish gleamed in the light. He marveled at the fact that what was once a pile of scraps was now a custom board all his own.

Gus, meanwhile, exhaled. "I thought that was going to go way worse."

"Where are your paints for the deck?" Bridger asked, looking around.

"Up in my room," Gus replied. "Should we go?"

Bridger lifted his eyebrows and gave a fast nod, eager to see what they could create.

Sleepover

Like habit, Gus opened the skinny door to his attic bedroom, and the boys walked in one after the other. Bridger glanced around, his face slowly brightening as he soaked in the private space. Gus had framed some of his favorite nature drawings, which now adorned the wooden walls. His sketching pencils and art supplies sat at the computer desk, which faced a starry window. Gus's cozy, sage-blanketed bed was illuminated gently by an heirloom lamp that gave the room a warm noir glow. He was so relieved that he had switched out his cowboy bedding his first week.

Bridger passed by a small boxy TV perched on a stand that held a sparse VHS collection of classic movies. The shelf also displayed an assortment of colorful pebbles, jagged rocks, and bundled twigs from varying Montana trees.

"Sorry, I don't have much," Gus sheepishly apologized. "I kinda just filled the room with whatever I could find around the cabin."

But Bridger's face seemed to reveal he was anything but let

down. He tilted his head back to see twinkling lights strung along the attic's rafters. Gus followed his gaze.

"These old Christmas lights were in those." Gus gestured toward a few dusty cardboard boxes still neatly tucked in the corner. "I bet my dad hasn't hung them since I was a kid. Some of the bulbs don't even work anymore."

"Damn... I wish my room was this cool," Bridger remarked.

Gus chuckled.

In the starry moonlight of the open window, the boys sat at Dan's oak desk with the clunky jewel-toned Apple computer. Gus lifted Bridger's polished but unpainted board onto his lap.

"What kind of design do you want?" Gus asked, pulling out his acrylics.

"Flames!" Bridger blurted out.

Gus nodded. He leaned toward his computer and searched for a few examples he thought Bridger might like.

"There! Like that one, but better. You can do better, yeah?"

Gus grinned. "Yeah."

He applied a shadowy background to Bridger's deck, upon which he painted streaks of fire using varying deep reds, amber oranges, and vibrant yellows. Bridger peacefully observed Gus's eyes and hands ebbing and flowing as he expertly brushed the colors across the slick wood grain. Bridger could only describe Gus doing art like he'd describe himself skating. *It just feels right. Natural.* A few minutes in, as Gus moved to create wisps at the edges of the flames, Bridger got an idea. Reaching into his pocket, he pulled out his MP3 player and started some music. Bridger placed one earbud in his own ear and reached over to put the other in Gus's.

As Bridger's fingers grazed his ear, Gus glanced up, surprised by the intimate touch. The computer's bright display and the starlight coming through the window cast a dreamlike glow over the two as Gus caught Bridger's smirk and slowly smiled. Both boys bobbed to the music together. Gus dipped his brush in a gold blend he'd mixed, and painted some more strokes of the fire, his beautiful design taking shape. Bridger swayed to the tunes and watched Gus fill in each and every detail. Soon the shadowy inferno was fully finished.

Bridger reached for his new skateboard and inspected it with awe. Gus smiled with satisfaction. "Should be dry by morning."

"How'd you learn all this art stuff?" Bridger inquired. "How are you so good at... everything?"

Gus's chest lifted at the compliment. Then his face slowly drooped as he looked down toward his feet.

"My mom... She was the real artist," Gus shared, tilting his gaze back up. His eyes settled on the bitterroot painting on his wall. "I just wanna be as good as she was."

Bridger's brow furrowed as Gus leaned back in his chair seemingly lost in thought. He regretted having asked anything at all.

"I'm sorry you lost her," Bridger sympathized.

Gus shrugged slowly, then let his head fall. He looked over at Bridger and decided he trusted him enough to open up for once.

"When I draw... I think of her. She had a boring job she hated, I didn't like school. So we'd stay up late every night together just making... beautiful things," Gus revealed.

Bridger tilted his head and offered a supportive, melancholy smile. He leaned his board of flames against the wall near their feet to safely dry right next to Gus's homemade board. The flame and mountain designs glinted together in the lamplight. Bridger turned back to Gus, wanting to hear more.

"No one in my family ever went to college. No one traveled. She wanted me to be the first to have that option, to have a choice in what I did. Not to be stuck with a life like she had after leaving Dad," Gus continued.

"Wow," Bridger breathed before continuing. "She sounds great."

"She was." Gus slid down in his seat and laid his head on the back of his desk chair, thinking. His eyes went distant as memories flooded back to him. "She was *so* pretty... She had this long, reddish-blonde hair. It smelled like lavender," Gus remembered, then smiled. "She always snuck me into art galleries without paying. She loved bad romance movies and takeout food. Sang awful songs in the car at full volume."

Gus chuckled at the memories. Bridger scooted in closer,

earnestly gazing at Gus as he kept talking.

"She never lazily said my art was good and went on with doing whatever. She always looked at it, really looked at it, and gave me great advice to improve something. I loved that."

Gus cleared his throat and tried not to let his eyes water.

"When I couldn't sleep, we'd share pints of cookie-dough ice cream at midnight... I miss that." His voice trailed off.

Bridger's eyes held a sensitive stare. He leaned forward and rapped on Gus's knee. "I wish I could have met her."

Gus nodded at Bridger. He paused, then turned to the dusty boxes in the corner.

"Actually. I think..." Gus stood up. "I think we might have old tapes in the attic here somewhere. Hold on..."

Gus stepped toward the corner of his bedroom while Bridger watched with hopeful curiosity. Gus shifted around boxes until he found a small one labeled *Megan's Home Movies.*

"I can't believe Dad kept these," Gus laughed, glad he had avoided tearing up too much.

After bringing the small box closer to Bridger at the desk, Gus fished out one of the old cassette tapes and pushed it into his TV's VCR slot. He pulled one of the top blankets off his bed and sat on the soft, faded patterned rug on the wooden floor, wrapping himself in the warm fabric of the blanket. As the first video started playing on the boxy screen, Bridger got up from his chair and snuck over to sit with Gus on the floor. They bumped shoulders. Gus glanced over, keenly aware of their closeness.

Gus and Bridger watched scenes Dan must have filmed over a decade ago featuring Megan and a young Gus. Gus's mom did indeed have pretty strawberry blonde hair, freckles dotting her kind face, and a bright captivating laugh that lit up Gus's dark bedroom. Both boys smiled as they watched baby Gus run around the yard outside, his mom waddling behind in chase. A fresh-faced Dan flipped bratwursts on the grill.

There was footage of Gus eating some birthday cake, of Megan painting a lake landscape on a large easel in Dan's woodshop with Gus play-painting beside her, of toddler Gus squeezing two tubes of oil paint all over himself *and* the living room couch.

Dan's and Megan's laughs echoed through the attic as they caught him.

"Oh no! What did you do, Gus?" Megan cooed. *"Show us what you did."*

"I w-ike colors!" toddler Gus chirped back.

Megan looked right up at her husband, her gaze slightly off-center from the camera lens. She smiled wide, her infectious giggle echoing through the TV speakers. Her eyes sparkled when she laughed.

Gus missed those eyes so much.

"See. She's the best." Gus pointed out to Bridger, then caught himself. "Or *was* the best."

Bridger nodded.

The boys kept going through the cassette tapes Dan had saved, watching childhood memories Gus had forgotten. Gus found himself wishing he had thought about the tapes sooner.

With the shimmering blue TV light reflecting off them both, the sounds of laughter on the screen, and the tiny twinkling Christmas bulbs above, the room had an electric charge. Bridger's bouncing knee brushed Gus's thigh and his skin warmed with gentle heat. Gus couldn't help himself from slowly glancing over at him. The skater boy was still facing the TV. Gus studied Bridger's face. *Why did he want to sleep over? His friends ditched me yesterday.* Gus looked away as reality sunk in. *He got his new board. After he takes it home tomorrow... are we done?*

In the video, Megan grabbed the camcorder from her husband and pointed the lens back at Dan. He cackled with so much joy, Gus almost didn't recognize this man as his father.

"Ha. Dude. When your dad laughs, he looks just like you." Bridger nudged Gus, and another bolt of electricity fired through him.

"What?" Gus looked over, ignoring the buzz in his legs. "You think?"

Bridger paused the video.

"Yeah. Look!"

"No way."

"Gus. Be serious. You guys have the same smile, same dimples." Bridger lifted a finger to Gus's face. It stopped a breath away to point at his cheek. He smirked. "That same lost look with doe eyes when you get confused."

Gus paused at Bridger's words. *He's watching me that closely? Are doe eyes bad?* Gus grunted a *hmph* and inspected his dad's face on the screen. "I guess." He shook his head. "But he's not like that anymore."

Later, as they were about to finish the last of the home movies, Bridger started yawning.

"Want the bed? I can take the floor." Gus offered, standing up.

"Nah, man. It's your room." Bridger waved casually. "I'll just take these and crash here."

Bridger grabbed the extra duvet folded up on Gus's mattress and laid it beside Gus's bed. He reached for the small blanket they'd used while watching the home movies, made it his cover, and tossed one of Gus's pillows to the ground. Gus switched off his lamps. The room went dark save for the soft twinkle lights in the rafters and a beam of moonlight slipping through the window.

"Can I take my shirt off?" Bridger asked in the dim quiet. "I sleep hot."

What? Gus stopped where he stood beside his bed. "Oh. Sure. Yeah," Gus responded.

"My jeans too?"

"Um, yeah." *Please stop asking.*

Bridger lifted the hem of his shirt and yanked it upward.

Gus's heart sped up as his eyes darted to scan Bridger's naked torso before he could even tell himself to look away. Twisting around with his back to Gus, Bridger unzipped and pulled down his jeans. He was wearing boxers with cartoon skulls on them. Gus blushed. Bridger turned back forward and Gus averted his gaze. He needed to get into bed and stop staring.

"Night, man. See you in the morning," Bridger said with a yawn. As Bridger stretched wide, Gus snuck another peek at Bridger's muscles as they flexed with his body's extensions. Gus looked away again.

Bridger lowered to the ground and whispered, "Can't wait to rock the new board at the park tomorrow."

Gus anxiously slid into his bed, pulled the sage covers over himself, and stared at the ceiling in quiet reflection. The starry night sky gleamed in the window behind him. Overly tense and trying to force himself to fall asleep, Gus lay in agony. His mind raced.

What was that sound?

Can he hear me breathe?

However, minutes later, Bridger was already snoring. Gus finally exhaled the stress of having someone else in his room. He quietly rolled to his side. His eyes stayed closed for a good while, but sleep never came. After more stretched minutes of overthinking, Gus opened his eyes again and peeked through the emptiness across his room, hyperaware of Bridger below. Gus's jaw tightened as his thoughts churned. He knew he shouldn't, but he couldn't help himself. Quiet as a snail, he inched to the edge of his bed and peered down at Bridger on the floor.

The boy was fast asleep, breathing deeply. Indeed sleeping hot, Bridger had pushed off his second blanket cover, revealing his bare torso and his underwear. He had hairy tufts under his armpits, defined biceps and abs, and the dazed slack-jawed expression of someone completely lost in slumber. Gus felt drawn to Bridger in a way he couldn't describe. Especially tonight, especially now. Gus studied Bridger's shirtless form in the moonlit darkness: his relaxed shoulders, firm chest muscles, the speckles of hair near his belly button, the curved outline in his boxers. He was tempted to leave his bed to join Bridger on the floor, to find out how firm Bridger's muscles were, to feel how warm he really was...

What am I doing? Gus snapped back to the center of his bed. He turned onto his side, facing away from Bridger. *Get a grip, Gus.*

A half hour later, full of shame, Gus finally fell asleep.

The next morning, while the boys ate scrambled eggs and waffles cooked by Dan, they chatted more about the possibility of selling boards to their friends. Dan seemed reluctant, but he couldn't turn down potential business.

"Are you positive kids your age will actually buy handmade boards?" Dan questioned the boys from the stove.

"Well, possibly?" Gus answered. "Some of Bridger's friends said—"

"Hell yes!" Bridger interrupted, already too comfortable in Gus's house. "All we gotta do is get the word out."

"How do we do that?" Gus asked.

"Already have a plan." Bridger winked at Gus as he scarfed down the last of his breakfast.

Gus quickly looked down at his food.

Bridger pointed up at Gus's father as he came to the table. "These waffles are killer!"

Dan released the smallest of grins as he put two more on the boy's plate. Bridger doused them in syrup and chugged his orange juice.

The boys scurried up to Gus's room. Bridger brought his waffles with him.

Up in the attic once again, Bridger grabbed Gus's board and put it on the desk as Gus started up his computer. Bridger then pulled out an old camera from his backpack.

"A camera? Where'd you get that?" Gus asked.

"It's from our basement. My dad says he wants to learn photography, but he hasn't touched this thing in five years," Bridger replied.

Bridger turned the camera around to face him and Gus. He stuck out his tongue like a rockstar and Gus rushed to grin awkwardly. The flash of the camera startled Gus. Bridger laughed at his friend's jumpiness. Gus blushed. He wasn't used to this—this closeness with a stranger, this ease between two. The camera snapped again.

"Okay, enough!" Gus pushed Bridger away with a chuckle. "Focus on the skateboards."

Bridger grinned as he next captured a photo of Gus's board, then his own, then Gus's sketchbook, where Gus had drawn a logo that read *SCRAPS* in all caps:

"The guys are gonna flip," Bridger celebrated.

A few minutes later, the logo and photos of Gus's board had loaded onto the computer screen. Bridger squeezed to sit with Gus on his small wooden desk chair. They each shared half of the same seat. *Why's he so close?* Gus wavered as Bridger started rearranging the photos on the computer into a simple advertisement.

"You sure you know what you're doing?" Gus questioned. "I could ask Tara. She knows computers better than us."

"Dude. We just pair these photos of our boards with your logo and boom! Business," Bridger explained.

"So... what? Kids look for us and ask about the boards?" Gus wondered.

"No, they call your dad's shop and buy one. Again, Gus. *Business.*" Bridger's arm danced in the air before descending to dramatically press print.

Gus rolled his eyes and turned to the printer as Bridger's flyer inched from the machine. It had the logo, pictures of their boards, a price list, and Dan's company phone number. Bridger proudly grabbed the flyer and gave it a flick. "Bus—"

"Business, yes, I get it." Gus elbowed him. He took the flyer and looked it over, nodding in feigned approval. It had the essentials but no artistic flair. His face scrunched up before he could stop it.

"What?" Bridger asked. "No good?"

"Uh..." Gus let out. "Let me add better designs."

Bridger gave Gus's shoulder a gentle shove. "Okay, Picasso. Let's see what you've got."

Later that morning, the boys drove to McNair Skatepark and stapled copies of Gus's new and improved flyer onto every nearby utility pole, wall, and wide tree trunk within a mile radius. When Avery, Bennet, and Coop arrived at the park without Max, Bridger slapped a flyer against each of his friends' chests.

"Bridge! You got a board, too?" Avery questioned eagerly as the other boys read the flyer. "Nice flames!"

His friends inspected his new board and roused each other up with excitement.

"Yeah!" Bridger tapped it with pride. "If you buy one, Gus and his dad can make anything."

Gus opened his mouth to protest *anything*, but the crew's wave of excitement crested, so he let it go."

"Could they do a wolf?!" Coop jumped in.

"I want a milf in a bikini!" Bennet added.

Avery and Coop announced "We're in!" in unison and dapped Bridger up, then turned to Gus to offer the same. Gus smiled, surprised, and dapped them back. The skaters' handshake was awkward, but Gus got through it.

They like me!

"We're crashing Max's bonfire tomorrow night after skating. Wanna come?" Coop invited.

"Hell yeah, we do!" Bridger accepted without a second thought.

From across the parking lot, Max Stevens exited his pickup and spotted Bridger, Avery, Coop, and Bennet skating. That loser Gus followed behind them.

"Psh."

As he walked closer to the park's edge, Max spotted a new flyer beside the entrance. He squinted, suspicious, and went over to read the paper.

"*Scraps*? The hell?"

He saw the picture of Gus's board and cursed, ripping the flyer from the post and tearing it apart. The shreds crumpled under the wheels of his board as he skated away from the park.

Chapter 8

The Bonfire

After meeting an hour away from town, Bridger led Gus on foot through the rural mountainous woods on the outskirts of Livingston. It was well beyond dusk. The moon peeked through the trees as twigs cracked underneath Gus as he followed Bridger through the brush and up a tall hill. A cabin's clearing came into view, and the boys could hear music and laughter. They'd thought they'd be too early, but Gus could already see throngs of teenagers dancing, vibing, drinking alcohol, and chatting around a raging bonfire. Coop, Bennet, and Avery brightened when they saw Bridger.

"Finally! Bridge, look! Max bought us all beers!" Bennet exclaimed, raising a Hamm's bottle as the boys walked their way. Bridger grabbed a beer from Coop for himself and stood next to his friends around the firepit. Gus tried to squeeze near the boys as they all chatted and drank, even as random strangers kept pushing between them. Eventually, their group settled down on some large rocks closer to the fire. Peering around, Gus crossed his legs and

87

bounced his knee nervously. Was everyone else really so comfortable around all these adult-looking partygoers they didn't know? Lots of college-aged guys wandered around in work boots, Wrangler jeans, and plaid shirts. Older girls in oversized sweaters wore lots of make-up for being so far in the woods this late at night. Several people in a huddle cheered and chugged their drinks in celebration as a stumbling guy in their midst finished a keg stand. It was... intense.

Why am I here?

Laughter from Bridger's friends pulled Gus back to their conversation.

"And then, when Mr. Winkler caught me with the exam answers, I was like, *Do you really wanna spend three whole months with me?*" Bridger recounted. "*Summer school sounds more like a punishment for you! Let's just let this one slide, Jeremy...*"

Everyone chuckled again. Bridger was such a natural at winning people over. Gus admired that charm, how easily Bridger commanded attention. As Bridger soaked in his moment of adoration, he caught Gus's eye. Bridger smirked and winked at him.

At that moment, a slower song started up, and the group of teens behind Gus tipsy-swayed to the music.

"Guys! Tara and her friends showed up," Avery announced.

All the boys whipped their heads around to see Tara Shae and her effortlessly pretty friends strolling past Max and his older drinking buddies.

"They could stomp on me and I'd say thank you," Bennet said, practically drooling.

"Tara's into Gus," Bridger whispered to the guys. "She chatted him up four times now."

It was three, only three!

"No way, dude!" Coop snapped back.

"Tara Shae," Avery started, "likes *Gus*?!"

All of Bridger's friends scanned Gus up and down.

"It's true! Gus, show 'em! Go talk to her," Bridger urged, nudging Gus's shoulder.

Gus went stark white. "What... now? I don't think I—"

"It's now or never," Coop insisted.

"I dare you. Do it," Bennet added.

"Double dog," Avery challenged.

"Gus! Go over to her," Bridger pushed.

"I'm not—"

Bennet stood up suddenly. "Wait, you'll look like an asshole without a beer." He cracked open a Hamm's and pressed the cold bottle into Gus's hand. "Okay. Go make us proud!"

Gus reluctantly stood up under the weight of the dare.

"Gus! Gus! Gus!" The boys all chanted quietly, encouraging him. *"Gus! Gus! Gus!"*

Gus cautiously walked over to Tara, who was holding a pilsner and laughing with her girlfriends. She spotted Gus and offered a little wave as he approached. Tara stepped to the side to chat with him.

"Um. Hi, Tara," Gus greeted nervously.

"Hey, Gus." Tara smiled back, leaning in for a big hug.

Gus could hear the boys react with muffled hoots behind him as Tara touched him, and he hoped she didn't notice. He smiled and hugged back with his free arm, unsure of where to put his hand.

"I never figured you were the booze and bonfire type," Tara remarked over his shoulder.

"I'm not," Gus admitted as the hug ended. "Bridger and his friends invited me."

"Ah. That makes sense. And we can't turn down Bridger, now can we?" She gave Gus a knowing look.

Gus nodded along despite not fully getting what she was trying to hint at. "I guess not... Why did you come?"

"Max asked me," Tara said.

"Oh?" Gus glanced over at Max to see if he was watching him with Tara, but he was busy crushing a beer can under his foot. "I thought you hated all those skate guys."

"Only the dumb ones," Tara laughed. "I don't hate you."

There was a moment of silence. Tara's wide open beam smoothed to a gentler smile.

"You sorta remind me of... me," Tara shared.

Gus tilted his head and grinned back. *What does she mean by that?*

"And even though I probably should... I also don't hate Max." Tara shook her head in annoyance. If it was at herself or at Max, Gus wasn't sure. "I have to drop some hard news on him soon, so I felt guilty and said yes to coming."

"What hard news?"

"Well, I nailed my first interview! I have another one this Friday," Tara shared excitedly.

"That's awesome!" Gus brightened up. "But... why is that bad?"

"No, it's great! Just... if I do get the job, telling Max will be hard."

"Why? Are you two close?"

"Well, we grew up together. We... used to date... sorta." Tara rolled her eyes and fidgeted a bit. "I think he still has a thing for me?"

"Really? I'd never guess that. You dating him, I mean. He's kind of aggressive."

"Exactly." Tara sighed. "After his dad died, Max became even more obsessed with skating. He stopped talking to friends, was being so cruel to everyone. Even me. So a few months later, before I started college, I broke up with him."

"Dang." Gus stared at his full beer. "I'm sorry."

"I'm not. It was gonna happen eventually. Even if he'd stayed nice like when we were kids," Tara reasoned. "I still care about him though."

"Why *happen eventually*?" Gus asked, puzzled.

Tara stared at Gus. She slowly grew a smirk again. Gus still had a blank look on his face. Tara crossed her arms and glanced around to ensure no one was watching them. Then she leaned in close.

"Have you not figured it out yet?" Tara whispered. "I thought that's why you and I bonded."

Gus still looked lost. *Is she actually into me?*

"Gus... I don't like guys, I like girls. I'm gay," Tara murmured with a laugh.

Gus's mouth slowly fell open and his head leaned back in realization. Everything clicked. He suddenly understood why she kept hinting about his friendship with Bridger.

Gus had no idea how to react.

"Wait. Do you think... Do you think that—that *I'm*...?" Gus stammered, unsure.

"Oh! Well, maybe I was wrong, but I just thought with Bridger..." Tara trailed off.

Gus turned to look at Bridger and his friends near the bonfire. They were still surveying him as if he were their brave pioneer exploring the uncharted world of hot college girls. Bridger was watching the closest of all.

"Oh... he actually just sent me over here to ask you out," Gus confessed awkwardly.

"What? Why?" Tara asked, surprised.

"They all dared me to," Gus explained.

"God! Boys are *so* dumb. But Bridger? He likes you. At least... in some sort of way."

Gus took a deep breath, not having expected the conversation to go this way. His shoulders lifted with skittish energy as his mind raced back through his interactions with Bridger and raised all kinds of questions about how the boy felt about him.

"You like him too, right? More than you've liked other friends before?" Tara asked.

"What? No. Well... I don't know what—" Gus stuttered. "...I didn't know that was an option."

And without warning, there was Max, a beer in hand and already stinking of booze. He stepped up next to Tara and shot Gus a look so intense it felt as though vicious darts were shooting his way. Immediately, Gus tensed up.

"What are *you* doing here?" Max sneered. He wore an unzipped greasy Carhartt hoodie over his shirtless torso. "Trying to sell your shitty decks?"

"No, I—"

"I saw the lame-ass flyers," Max spat out, his speech slurred, as he pushed forward into Gus's personal space.

"I was invited by Aver—"

"Get lost. No one wants you here, especially not Tara," Max growled.

Tara turned to Max, offended but remaining calm.

"Yes, I do. I want Gus here," she asserted.

Max scoffed, looking baffled as to how scrawny Gus could win over his old girlfriend. "You're into this wimpy art freak?"

Tara stepped closer to Max, looked up into his eyeballs, and poked his chest. "Stop that," she defended. "If you send Gus home, I go home."

Max's eyes sharpened and jumped from Gus to Tara and back again, confusion and jealousy creeping in. He took a long swig of his beer before saying anything.

"Fine. Whatever. Why is everyone being so lame lately?" Max muttered as he twisted away and walked off, visibly annoyed.

Gus grinned at Tara. He had never been defended like that. Tara clinked her beer against his.

The sky faded to inky black and the bonfire's embers burned low. Most of Max's college-aged friends had either paired off with girls to make out in the woods or, if they had been unsuccessful, headed home. Max was fully necking a girl by a tree. Coop interrupted Gus and Bridger, who were chatting by the fire, to deliver important news. A girl stood behind him, her hand outstretched toward his while she said her goodbyes to friends. Coop looked to ensure her back was turned.

"Dudes, me and Rachel are gonna..." Coop thrust his hips back and forth crudely while trying to be lowkey so Rachel wouldn't notice. "See ya at the skatepark tomorrow."

Bridger shook his head and playfully mouthed, "Asshole." As Rachel twisted around to face them, Bridger immediately switched to a positive demeanor and raised his beer to the departing couple.

"Have fun!" Bridger laughed.

Coop smirked as he turned around with Rachel to walk off, leaving Gus and Bridger with Bennet and Avery. About five minutes later, Avery stood up. Bennet followed suit.

"Well, I'm goin' home before my parents find out what I did tonight," Avery announced.

"Yeah, every girl here turned me down, so I'm gonna peace out too," Bennet conceded.

Gus and Bridger shared looks and a shrug.

"Okay. We're gonna finish our drinks here," Bridger said while adding another log to the fire.

Gus nodded his agreement.

All the boys slap-shook goodbye. Avery and Bennet walked away, leaving Bridger and Gus alone by the bonfire.

The boys continued to chat, eat s'mores, swig drinks, and laugh long into the night. Soon almost everyone else had left the bonfire. Only one remaining drunk teen could be heard barfing behind a nearby tree. Everyone else had gone into the forest or back home.

"My ass is sore from these rocks." Bridger stood up from the fire. "Come here."

Bridger grabbed a blanket that someone had left behind and spread it out wide over the grass in front of a log, still near the fire. He then picked up two fresh beers and sat down on the blanket. Gus stepped over to join Bridger, realizing as his legs wobbled underneath him that he was a little tipsy even from his light drinking. As he sat down, they both leaned back against the log. Now much more relaxed, the boys turned toward the stars above them.

Bridger reached over, grabbed Gus's old beer, and downed the rest.

"Hey!" Gus laughed. "I wasn't done with that."

"You're always too slow." Bridger smirked and offered Gus one of the unopened beer bottles. "You gotta catch up."

Gus took the drink. Bridger reached for a bottle opener in his back pocket, which he used to pop open both of their icy brews. Bonfire sparks flew up with the smoke before them. Bugs buzzed. Gus listened to the wind whishing through the nearby trees and realized they were now fully alone. Gus checked the time on his Casio.

"It's 2:00 a.m. How am I not tired?" Gus questioned.

"'Cause it was a great party." Bridger looked at Gus, then huffed. "But now everyone's sleeping—or screwing! I'm jealous!"

Gus chuckled. Both boys paused to taste their new beers. It was calmer now.

"Thanks for bringing me," Gus broke the silence. "It's cool you have so many friends."

"I dunno if I'd call them all *friends*," Bridger responded, "but they're pretty cool, I guess."

"But... *we're* friends, right?" Gus said, looking over at Bridger.

"Duh," Bridger replied with a happy scoff. "You're the best."

Gus smiled. *Is Tara right? I mean... he is treating me different.*

"Well," Gus ventured, "that's good, 'cause... I tell you things I've never told anyone. Not even my mom."

"Yeah, I don't tell my parents jack," Bridger agreed, watching the wisps of the bonfire.

There was a pause. Both boys took another sip of beer. Gus snuck a look at Bridger. *Do I like him* too *much? I don't want to... be gay... if he's not.*

Gus breathed deeply. He had to say something. Anything.

"Sometimes... I can't say *out loud* how I feel," Gus shared quietly. "To my parents, to friends... I just keep my mouth shut and put everything in my sketchbook. That world makes more sense to me. Even if what I draw isn't real."

Bridger nodded slowly. He pulled his gaze away from the flames to turn to Gus.

"That sounds lonely," Bridger observed.

"Yeah..." Gus dropped his head, looking at the fire, lost in sad thought.

Bridger scanned Gus, squinting in slight concern. Gus was shrinking inward.

"I think I've kinda gotten used to being alone," Gus admitted. "Especially this year."

Bridger brought his legs in and tilted his head with a big grin. He tapped Gus on the knee. "But, I mean, hey! You're gonna make tons of new friends at your big new school, right?"

Gus stayed still. The logs in the fire crackled. He shook his head. "I doubt it. Nothing lasts if you have to leave."

Another log in the fire spit embers.

"Maybe I stay here," Gus blurted, suddenly facing Bridger. "Keep working in the shop."

"What?" Bridger joined Gus's tense, worried gaze. "No. You can do so much better than here."

"But what if I never find a friend like you again?" Gus asked softly.

Bridger turned away.

Gus again faced the fire. *Damn. Why'd I say that?*

"Look, at least you have opportunities. I'm good at skating, sure. But beyond skating...?" Bridger lifted his beer bottle and gestured into the distance. "Well, there is no beyond. Every day kinda feels the same."

Bridger picked up a twig and snapped it between the fingers of one hand, growing more serious.

"I haven't even thought about my future. Ever." Bridger shook his head. "You're the first person who's ever made me think about that stuff."

Gus focused on Bridger's subtle movements, on his body language, unsteady in a way Gus had never seen before.

Is he nervous?

"Well... what do you want?" Gus asked, trying to smile.

Bridger scoffed. "I mean, being a virgin kinda sucks, so getting laid would be pretty nice."

Both boys laughed. Bridger dug his foot into the grass. Gus watched him.

"But seriously. What do you want?" Gus said quietly again.

Bridger looked up as he pondered.

Could he want...

"I don't know," Bridger answered finally. "Get a good job? Make some money. Buy a kickass car?" He chuckled, watching the flames. "Probably a girlfriend, too. Right?"

Gus's laughing smile dropped. His eyes slowly drifted down.

I knew it. A girl.

"Yeah..." Gus responded softly. "Me too..."

Bridger shrugged and tapped his beer, still pondering his life.

"But do *I* really want those things? My parents have all that stuff and they're still miserable, so..." Bridger trailed off.

"Yeah, my parents both ended up sad, too," Gus agreed.

"See?! It's too complicated," Bridger concluded. He sighed and turned back to Gus. "Man, life is hard. And the future stresses me out. All I can handle is now," he said, leaning in close to Gus and lifting his drink slightly.

"And right now," Bridger added, "I'm happy."

He nodded as if to confirm that statement to himself, looking out at the night sky before them with a soft smile.

Gus also leaned back. His shoulder brushed Bridger's, but he held it there. Bridger didn't pull away. They were very close. Heat radiated between their bodies.

Gus smiled nervously and asked, "Do you even... want a girl-friend?"

Bridger nodded but then paused to re-think for a moment.

"I've never had anyone like me like that. Not really," Bridger responded honestly.

Gus blinked at Bridger and shook his head. "You will though. You're attractive."

Bridger spit beer back into his bottle.

"You think I'm hot?" Bridger snorted. He drunkenly leaned into Gus, playfully nudging his shoulder.

Both boys laughed again.

"Hey! I never said *hot*!" Gus rebuffed, trying to hide his nerves with a wide, joking grin.

Bridger's smile faded. He squinted in curiosity.

"What do you want in a girl, Gus?" Bridger asked.

Gus sniffed in indifference before realizing Bridger was being serious. He paused to think as Bridger looked back into the fire.

"I don't know..." Gus admitted.

He stole a slow, secret yearnful glance at Bridger. "Someone who makes me laugh. Someone who supports me, believes in me. Someone I can be myself around," Gus responded, searching Bridger's eyes from the side. "You?"

Bridger breathed in and thought hard.

"A girl who wants me *for me*, you know? A real connection. Someone who inspires me to try new things. Makes me do my best. Someone who goes on adventures. Like..."

Bridger lifted his drink up to the sky. His eyes twinkled as he looked over at Gus, who grew a grin.

"Nights like these! Getting drunk under the stars at 2:00 a.m. Making out by a warm campfire." Bridger nodded in tipsy delight.

Gus raised his eyebrows. *Is he joking or... serious?*

"Don't be getting any ideas," Gus teased with a shaky laugh.

Bridger rolled his eyes playfully and softly hit Gus in the arm.

"Shut up!" he joked, staring at Gus longer than normal.

Both boys paused in their happy state, locking eyes.

The air suddenly felt different. They were now so close, they could almost hear each other's quickening heartbeats. Warmth grew from more than just the fire. Bridger chuckled and looked deeply at Gus, who flicked his head away and swigged his beer. Bridger glanced down to watch Gus's lips as he drank.

There was a pause. Gus peered back at the silent Bridger, who immediately averted his gaze. Bridger took a long deep breath, as if to convince himself of something. He downed his beer, then leaned in very close to Gus's face. Bonfire reds and moonlight blues illuminated him as he released a vulnerable, tipsy confession.

"Gus," Bridger spoke softly, "if you were a girl, I'd kiss you right now."

Those words made Gus choke on his next thought. Milliseconds became minutes as Bridger looked directly into his eyes. Gus's heart pumped harder than it ever had before. His breath became shorter, goosebumps swept across his skin, his cheeks flushed. Everything inside Gus became one single thought:

Do it. Kiss me now.

The sounds of nature that had filled their silence faded away. Gus, scanning between Bridger's own darting eyes, tilted his head, his brow raised in desire. He warmed up with an anxious tipsy smile. Bridger finally leaned closer. They were separated only by inches.

Gus dared to move forward.

Kiss me.

Bridger scoffed with gentle remorse and pulled his head away from Gus.

"But that would be... gay, right?" he whispered.

The bonfire's smoky winds of regret blew back in as reality solidified in Gus's undrawn world.

Gus's heart sank as Bridger laughed off the awkward moment. *Was he joking this whole time?*

Bridger leaned on the log behind them again, grabbed another bottle of nearby beer, and looked back up at the stars. Gus didn't know how Bridger was so fully unfazed by what had just happened.

Because it's ridiculous. He'd never kiss me, Gus reflected. *We're not those kinds of guys.*

Turning his own gaze to the stars, Gus yawned as his pained heartbeat slowed back down. He drank the last drops of beer in his bottle and clenched his teeth, lost in the constellations.

What's wrong with me?

Gus didn't know. But at least Bridger was still here. As the moment passed, Gus breathed in and decided he needed to accept things as they were. Bridger was his friend. That was it. That was all he could be.

Gus yawned again. Whether from the booze, the late-night talk, his busy day, or the adrenaline crash from the almost-kiss, Gus fell asleep right there, next to the bonfire's dead embers, without realizing it.

In the morning, when Gus awoke, he was still in the same spot in the forest. He sat up and looked around.

Bridger was gone.

Chapter 9

Mornings After

Max Stevens and two of his older skate friends lay passed out in Bridger's sporty bedroom with skate posters on the wall and used clothes scattered across the floor. Boozy drool leaked from Max's open mouth as he snored. Crushed beer cans littered the carpet. Bridger groaned as he woke, rolling over in his bed. His head was banging worse than his first skate crash.

Fuck. Last night.

Bridger struggled to get his feet out from his covers. He stepped past his conked-out friends and walked to his family bathroom.

As Bridger showered to wash off all the sweat, smoke, and dirt from the bonfire of just a few hours ago, all the memories of what transpired pitter-pattered back into his brain: the wild stories, the drinks, the girls, Gus—

Gus. Fuck... Bridger let his head sink under the shower's stream. *Shit. Why'd I say all that? Why'd he ask so much? Why does he care so much what I think? Why'd he look at me like... that?*

Bridger's breathing quickened with worry as he shut the water off and ripped the shower curtain open. He wiped the foggy mirror above the sink to see himself for the first time that morning. He stood naked, dripping wet, breathing heavily. He was hungover and stressed.

I almost...

Shit.

Bridger's eyes narrowed at his reflection, forcing himself to see reason. *I was drunk! That's why it was weird. He's a dude. I don't like dudes.* Bridger stared back at his own face, confused. Gus's joking about him not *getting any ideas* flashed back into his mind. Bridger shook his head. Locking lips with Gus by that bonfire would have been insane. Gus would have had that cute, dumb, surprised look he always had. Bridger scoffed. He couldn't resist a smile forming, imagining how funny it would have been to kiss Gus.

His little blue eyes, his woody smell, his taste...

Bridger caught his own mistaken smirk. *Fuck.* He glared in the mirror. *No... Who gives a shit? Nothing's gonna happen. Gus isn't like the other guys. He's different... but whatever. Doesn't mean I'm different. He always—*

"Dude! Let me in!" Max pounded on the bathroom door. "I gotta piss!"

Bridger flinched.

"Almost done, man!" Bridger sputtered in stress. "I'm—"

Max pushed the door open. Bridger jumped back in shock and wrapped a towel around his naked waist.

"Hey! I'm not ready ye—"

Max barged past Bridger holding a half-empty Hamm's. He spit into the toilet, unzipped his pants, and started to urinate right next to his friend.

Bridger recoiled. "Dude. What the fuck?!"

Max chuckled as Bridger averted his gaze from his crotch just in time—only to get a full view of Max's ass in the mirror as he peed. Bridger tightened up from the uncomfortable intrusion.

"The bitches were all over me last night," Max gloated.

Bridger stood awkwardly as Max glanced over at him with a

devilish grin. He looked away from the mirror.

Max's smile dropped, his pupils dilating as he eyed down Bridger's backside in the loose towel.

"We gotta leave soon or my parents will freak," Bridger said.

Max came back to himself. "Sure, I'll hose off quick, dude."

Bridger exited the bathroom and closed the door.

Max was left alone. His pants were still unzipped. He could hear Bridger shaking his friends awake, but Max didn't speed up. Still hungover, Max crept toward the mirror, off-balance. He noticed Bridger's toothbrush near the sink, inspected it, and grew antsy for a prank. He poured his leftover beer over the bristles and brushed his own teeth with Bridger's toothbrush, chuckling to himself.

Max's slow drunken gaze clocked Bridger's dirty clothes on the bathroom floor as he returned Bridger's toothbrush. His friend's used boxers topped the little heap. Max stiffened. He looked back at himself in the mirror with hesitation. *Fuck!* Max twisted away and turned on the shower. He slowly leered back at Bridger's dirty underwear again. *Fuck...*

Max pulled off his shirt and cracked his neck, thinking. He dropped his shirt and it hit the floor right next to Bridger's pile of dirty clothes. Max breathed groggily as one hand reached into his own pants and his other stretched down and scooped up Bridger's used boxers. He slowly lifted the underwear to his face and took a deep, slow whiff.

Fuck.

After waking up in the forest with no other partygoers around, Gus had to find his own way back to his dad's car and drive himself home. So many questions ping-ponged around his brain as he rode back down the rural roads. He was furious and growing more overwhelmed with each passing mile.

Did he really just leave me in the forest all alone?

Who does that?
We didn't even do anything...
Maybe it's my fault? Did I ask him too much?
There's no way he actually would have kissed me.
But he almost did...

The blaring sun beat down as Gus parked in his father's driveway and walked toward the cabin, still stuck in his own head. However, as he passed the woodshop, Dan stepped out from the barn door.

"Where've you been?" Dan asked his son with a straight face.

Gus cringed and turned back around. *Crap.*

"Just out for a morning drive," Gus fibbed.

"Don't lie to me." Dan crossed his arms. "We said no more secrets."

Gus sighed. He couldn't tell his dad everything, not when he'd freak so easily.

"I went to a bonfire," Gus half-shared. "With Bridger's friends. It was chill."

Dan waited for Gus to elaborate more. Gus didn't. Father and son stared at each other. Dan looked disappointed. Gus knew that look well. He was disappointed in himself, too.

"Did you drink?" Dan probed.

"...Only a little," Gus settled on, hoping his dad would buy it.

"You're underage."

Gus laughed lightly. "Yeah, but—"

"You could have crashed driving back."

"But I didn't."

"Gus." Dan shook his head. "I raised you better than this."

Gus jutted his chin up, angry now. *Is he joking?*

"You didn't *raise* me." Gus gave a dejected glare back. "Mom did."

These words halted Dan. He nodded with regret and slight contempt. He took a step back and moved his hands to hook them into his belt, frustration pouring in fast.

Gus looked away, irritated. He just wanted to be alone to think.

"I should have," Dan relented when Gus began walking away.

"I should have helped out more."

Gus glanced back at that admission. However, his father's upset grimace still remained.

"You're smarter than this, Gus."

"I know."

Dan gestured to how disheveled Gus looked. "Go clean up."

"Fine," Gus agreed.

Gus turned and walked up the porch stairs of their cabin. He opened the door.

"Hey," Dan called out before Gus stepped inside.

The boy looked back at his father standing alone out in their front yard.

"I'm glad you're safe," Dan said quietly.

Gus nodded without a care and walked inside. He should have said something back, but he didn't.

In the bathroom, Gus pulled off his smoky shirt and his jeans stained with wet grass and dirty charcoal. He showered under steaming hot water, attempting to wash his preoccupied misgivings away. Gus then lay down in bed and stared mindlessly at his ceiling. Since it was already midday, his usually twinkling lights above him were turned off. Without the small bulbs glowing beautifully, the long wrangling cords just looked like green snakes constricting the rafters above him. Gus felt squeezed and ensnared in his own head, too.

I've never felt this way about anyone before... any guy.

I want to kiss him... do more.

Gus turned from his wooden ceiling to the bedside trunk where his sketchbook sat. The thin box of colored pencils Bridger told him to use for his portrait lay on top. Gus grabbed both objects. He was tempted to sketch Bridger a thousand different ways, unable to stop seeing Bridger's face and all its minute expressions that were permanently etched into his mind after last night. However, Gus decided to use his colored pencils to document just one moment. The moment before Bridger leaned in to kiss him.

He was going to kiss me, right?

An hour later, as the close-up tipsy smile, red lips, swooping hair, and piercing deep amber eyes of Bridger took shape on Gus's page, Gus fell into his normal flow, wishing for what could never be. He imagined various scenarios of how last night could have gone. Right here in his sketchbook, Gus could *make* them all happen. But as Gus added in the final golden reflections from the bonfire on Bridger's dashing face, the fantasy of the moment lost its spark of potential.

Why can't this be real?

I want Bridger to look at me like this again... for real.

I shoulda just kissed him first! Been brave!

Gus let his head fall back, staring again at the strangled rafters.

But... I'd rather have him as a friend than nothing at all.

I can't scare him away. I have to be normal.

Last night didn't happen. I gotta forget it.

Gus peered down at the fictionally perfect Bridger before him. He smiled faintly but closed his sketchbook.

I gotta talk to him.

Gus placed his sketchbook back on the wooden trunk beside his bed and put on fresh clothes. He picked up his board from the corner of his room and dashed down the stairs.

Gus drove out to McNair Skatepark and, as he pulled into the gravel parking lot, immediately scanned the area for Bridger. His friend wasn't there.

He got out of the car and walked around.

He has to be here somewhere.

Gus scratched his head as he traversed the whole length of the park. The only people there right now were the cigarette girls sitting in their normal spot at the highest concrete bowl. Gus realized he was right now no different than the groupie girls, waiting around for the skate boys. He sighed.

Maybe he'll call the cabin. We can talk about what happened. Or not talk about it.

Then, like a storm cloud, Max's crew rolled up in a blue pickup truck. About five or six guys jumped out of the trunk.

Bridger was with them.

Shoot.

Gus retreated off the concrete near the picnic table by the south bowl. The boys rushed to the center of the park, Bridger at the rear and chipper as ever. Gus leaned in to try and overhear the skate guys as they stepped onto the pavement.

"I got with Kelly, Coop got with Rachel, and Bridger says he was up all night with Sophia. The one with HUGE tits," Max announced.

All the boys' jaws dropped in amazement as some of them uttered encouraging grunts, punched Bridger in the arm, or thrust their hips and laughed.

"Let's just say... I had a *great* night," Bridger bragged.

The guys all dapped him up, and Bridger glowed with pride.

Gus, eavesdropping from afar, shook his head.

He left me alone in the woods... for a girl?

The skaters all separated, dropping their boards and starting their various runs. Bridger, however, tucked his board under his arm and twisted in Gus's direction to use the water fountain.

Shit. Gus ducked and tried to hide, but Bridger had spotted him. The skater's gloating smirk faded. He ignored Gus and turned away from him to drink.

Just go talk to him.

And say what? Nice almost-kiss?

Gus shook his head. He and Bridger were friends. Last night, that was... nothing.

Gus stepped up to Bridger gingerly.

"Hey. Are you okay?" Gus asked. "I woke up this morning and didn't know where you went."

"Yeah. Sorry. I woke up to take a piss. Max found me and I had to bolt," Bridger replied.

"Okay..." Gus said. "Are... we good?"

"Yeah, man! No stress," Bridger assured him.

Gus nodded, but Bridger's smile felt different.

"So... did you really hook up with Sophia after I fell asleep?" Gus inquired.

Bridger's eyebrows raised, then his gaze narrowed. He paused for a moment. Bridger looked back at the guys to make sure they weren't close enough to hear their conversation.

"No. Alright?" Bridger gritted his teeth to whisper at Gus. "But I didn't want the guys asking questions about why I was still in the forest with you the whole night. So I lied to get them off my case."

The isolating shame of those first days at the park flashed back to Gus. His skin went hot. "Oh. Okay... fine," he replied.

Bridger sighed with regret as Gus's face fell.

"Look," Bridger explained, "I just can't let the guys get the wrong impression of you and me."

"And what impression would that be?" Gus questioned, leaning his head closer.

Bridger opened his mouth to mention something but then stopped himself.

Gus knew what he didn't want to admit. He shifted awkwardly on his feet waiting for Bridger to say something. *Does he not want to hang out with me anymore?*

But then Bridger took a deep breath and shared a forced small grin.

"It doesn't matter." Bridger pushed hair out of his face. "I don't want to think about it anymore. I just want to unwind."

Gus nodded. He took a step back and peered around, his eyes falling on the small lake across the park.

"Me too," Gus said. "And... I think I know a good place."

Bridger raised his eyebrows and tilted his head in curiosity. This time, he smiled wide.

Chapter 10
Our Own Little World

Gus and Bridger skated down the old paved road from Dan's property toward open pastures under the mountains. Gus pointed to the woods far in the distance. The boys kicked up their boards and, with Gus in the lead, trod together through a field of weeds and flowers. Fond memories of walking this remote path with his parents returned to Gus as they weaved through pine and spruce trees until a spring-fed lake was revealed.

"I used to come here with Mom and Dad," Gus shared. "We'd have picnics. Swim."

The hidden pristine lake had a short pebbly shore, and swooping branches hung over the water like a canopy. Big rocks, sturdy enough to stand on, dotted the spring. They led to a waterfall farther up the hill toward the mountain.

"The water's so clear," Bridger observed. "You can see the bottom."

Gus nodded. "Yeah. It's great for just floating like a leaf and thinking about nothing."

"That's what I need."

Bridger ripped off his shirt, eager to jump into the lake. Gus sat down on the ground and pulled out his colored pencils. He opened his journal to an in-progress drawing—a sparrow with a crooked wing next to unfinished flowers in some faded green grass.

Bridger stopped while crouching and taking off his shoes. He squinted at Gus's sketchbook. "Why's that bird's wing messed up?"

"Huh?" Gus looked over at his friend and raised an eyebrow. "Oh. Yeah. It's a sparrow. And the wing's broken."

"I can see that," Bridger said with a laugh. "I mean, why draw a broken bird stuck on the ground?"

Gus shrugged, placing down his pencil.

"I dunno. I love sparrows, and the image just came to my head."

"So this didn't actually happen?" Bridger squinted at the page. "Why bother drawing it?"

"Because I still care... I'm still curious," Gus explained, adding some sketched grass beneath the sparrow's feet. "What happens when little birds fall by mistake, get hurt, can't get off the ground?"

"Sucks to suck, I guess." Bridger stood back up. "That little guy will be eaten in no time."

Gus frowned playfully. "Hey, at least he can enjoy these purple flowers I drew for him. Even if he can't go anywhere... he still deserves something beautiful."

Bridger's joking face softened. "You're way too nice!" he finally concluded with a laugh. "How the hell did *we* become friends?!"

Gus looked up at Bridger with a lightheartedly defensive grin. "I'm not too nice! I just wanna see the sparrow fly again."

Bridger finished undressing down to his boxer briefs and tossed his pants aside.

"Okay. I'm gonna swim. You coming?" Bridger asked.

"Hmm... Next time." Gus tapped his sketchbook. "I'm gonna finish this."

Bridger shrugged with a smile, about to run off.

"Your loss, Bird Boy." He winked.

Gus stared after him.

With a yelp of unbridled joy, Bridger bolted into the cold lake and threw his arms through the water like propellers, splashing big and loud.

Gus couldn't help laughing as he watched him go. He shook his head with a warm smile. Gus then glanced back down at the bound parchment pages in his lap and continued sketching.

An hour later, Bridger was still floating in the spring like a lily pad. Gus was almost finished with his broken-winged sparrow amongst the forest flowers. Bridger climbed out of the water, dripping wet, onto a nearby rock. He stood up on the hard stone surface and leaned down to grab a small flat pebble.

"Gus! Watch this!" Bridger called out.

Gus lifted his gaze as Bridger wound up and grunted, throwing the rock as hard, high, and far as he could. Gus watched with confusion as the pebble flew and disappeared from sight. Bridger nodded with satisfaction.

Gus shook his head with a chuckle. "What?"

Bridger looked off into the distance. "No one can see us or hear us out here!" he announced, looking back at Gus. "We're in our own little world."

Gus smiled at the sweet thought and took a relaxing breath. Bridger sat down on the rock he was standing on and stretched out on his back to tan under the golden sun. There was complete silence; only pond and forest sounds resonated around two boys at peace in each other's presence.

Gus glanced over at Bridger in thought, flipping to a new page of his artbook. He grabbed some pencils of aqua, cerulean, emerald, burnt sienna, and harvest gold. He traced every colorful curve of Bridger's form over the mossy spring: the slope of his sunbathing chest and how it melted into his abs, the tufts of short brown hairs under the arms held behind his head. Long eyelashes hung from serenely closed eyes. Gus drew them in hickory brown. His defined jawline, now rendered in sable, held a smirk even while he rested. Gus could never tire of Bridger being his muse.

Time passed. Clouds rolled through in the sky above them.

Bridger, still sunbathing, peacefully drew his fingers through the water below him as his mind wandered. With a similar swirling hand, Gus put the final touches on his sketch, shading with his pencil. It was finished.

"You know... I love doing nothing with you," Bridger confessed in the silence.

Gus looked up. He smiled. "Yeah," Gus said in response. "With us, nothing feels... special."

A warmth filled Gus as he watched Bridger bob his head in agreement.

A drop of rain then hit Gus's sketchbook right on Bridger's copper cheek like a tear wetting the page. Gus peered toward the sky. Bridger rubbed a new droplet off his stomach, sitting up. One more hit Gus's shoulder. He locked shocked gazes with Bridger and closed his sketchbook. The drops became a drizzle.

"Shit!" Bridger exclaimed.

"No! We're so far out!" Gus replied anxiously.

Bridger got up off his rock and tiptoed across the stones back to where he'd dropped his clothes, rushing to clumsily put them back on. Gus zipped up his backpack and put on his shoes.

Skateboards overhead, the boys dashed out from the lake. Gus led their way as Bridger hopped behind, pulling up his pants with one arm. They ran through the forest, splashing through mushy sections of mossy ground. Dark storm clouds brewed overhead. Far off, a huge bolt of lightning pierced the evening sky.

When they finally got within sight of Gus's home, they were drenched. Rain ticked like marbles on the woodshed's metal roof as the boys hurried close, jumping over the puddles pooling in Dan's yard. They dropped their boards and rushed toward the shelter of Dan's workshop.

Bursting through the door, muddy and soaked to the bone, the boys were so cold their teeth chattered.

"Stay there! Don't get mud anywhere," Gus instructed as he shut the door, removing his shoes and grabbing a towel from a nearby bin.

Bridger turned to look at himself in a window pane and fixed his hair, still panting from running. He removed his soiled shoes and soaked, mud-splashed shirt. He stood there, wet and glistening, smudges of clay on his face. Then he yanked the towel away from Gus.

"Hey! I'm still using that!" Gus protested.

"You're muddier than I am. Let me use it before it's ruined," Bridger retorted, taking the towel.

Gus rolled his eyes. He took his shirt off shyly and wrapped it up for the laundry as Bridger dried himself off. Gus felt awkward standing there with no shirt. He checked the bin again. There were no other towels.

"Hurry up, I'm cold!" Gus urged.

Standing there shivering, Gus grabbed for the towel again. Bridger caught it before it fell. Both boys had a slight tug-of-war over the fabric. Bridger yanked the towel away again with a show of force and chuckled as Gus's grip failed.

"Asshole," Gus muttered timidly.

Gus eyed Bridger's body as he took his time wiping off. When Bridger looked over, Gus turned away.

Bridger smirked. He finished drying, stepped closer to Gus and, as if to crown a king, wrapped the towel around Gus's shoulders with a peaceful sigh.

"There. All yours," Bridger cooed, and patted Gus's head.

Standing still, hair damp, both boys smiled at each other, then chuckled.

The stare lasted too long. Their grins faded.

Bridger leaned forward and hastily kissed Gus.

Gus's eyes widened in surprise as Bridger's closed with carefree passion.

The kiss deepened, and Gus, subsumed by it all, relaxed into it, tilting his head.

Their breaths synced as their lips moved together, slow and searching. Bridger tugged on the damp towel wrapped around Gus's shoulders, pulling him closer, lifting him onto his toes.

A sudden crack of thunder shook the woodshop as lightning flashed outside the rain-streaked window behind the kissing boys.

Bridger jumped but didn't break away. Gus chuckled, smiling against Bridger's lips, and reached out to graze Bridger's bare chest to calm him.

Gus gave a last peck. Bridger pulled slowly away.

The boys, breathless in the moment, locked gazes.

"I... didn't mean to do that," Bridger said.

Gus said nothing. Instead, he leaned forward and stole another short kiss from Bridger, surprising himself.

When Bridger smiled, his eyes twinkling with joy, Gus smiled back.

This was real.

Exhaling all his fears, Bridger flashed a cheeky grin and dove back in to embrace Gus. The boys kissed passionately, deeper and deeper. Every new action they took happened naturally, their bodies moving for them. Bridger's hands slid around the small of Gus's back. Gus's arms wrapped around Bridger's shoulders and the towel fell to the floor. Bridger waddled them forward, pressing Gus up against the main worktable. Two-by-fours fell and clattered to the ground. The boys both laughed but didn't stop kissing, wouldn't stop kissing, *couldn't* stop kissing. The heat of them rose, even in the cold of the rainstorm. Sweat dripped from their backs, their chests, as they held each other close, as their lips found each other again and again. Gus felt stiffening in both their pants as Bridger pressed into him. Never had Gus felt so energized. He could kiss Bridger forever.

A distant door slam sounded outside the shop. Footsteps approached.

The boys parted immediately.

Dan walked into the dry workshop, his head covered with his jacket to hide from the downpour.

The boys separated even more, fearful of being found out.

Dan shook off his wet jacket and spotted the shirtless boys.

"Oh! Gus? Bridger?" Dan questioned. He evaluated them for a moment in which both boys were certain he knew.

Bridger turned to Gus, unsure of how to explain themselves.

Gus had never seen Bridger this terrified.

"You boys are soaked," Dan said. "Don't get water on the equipment."

"We just ran back from swimming in the lake. Didn't want to get hit by lightning," Gus explained quickly. Bridger stayed uncharacteristically silent.

"We're definitely rained in for the night," Dan agreed.

Dan turned away, taking off his wet jacket and boots. Bridger peered at Gus. They both smiled awkwardly, unsure of what to do next. Gus took a moment to think as Bridger looked down at his feet.

"Bison stew sound alright to you, Bridger?" Dan asked.

Bridger's smile faded as new regrets rushed in.

"Actually, I—I have to go," Bridger replied, heading toward the door and picking up his muddy shirt.

Gus was taken aback.

"In this mess?" Dan responded. "Okay."

Gus cleared his throat and walked toward Bridger as the boy rushed to put on his shirt and shoes.

"Hey, wait up," Gus whispered after him.

"I'll chat with you in the morning." Bridger grinned through the lie.

Something was off. This... shift in Bridger, like a flicked light switch. Gus didn't know what to do. Before he could do anything at all, Bridger escaped out the door and back into the rain. Gus watched Bridger pick up his skateboard through the window and run away with his head down.

"...Was it the bison stew?" Dan asked, breaking the silence.

Gus grimaced and closed his eyes, fearing that what happened tonight was yet another huge mistake.

Chapter 11

Two Broken Birds

The next day Gus was expected to work with his father on a wooden bench order for Gallatin County Regional Park in Bozeman. However, he was agitated with every task. Gus couldn't focus. While transferring lumber from their storage shed, he told himself Bridger *could* still call him later to make plans for the weekend.

He'll call. He wouldn't just... forget about me...

Gus kept telling himself this.

As the saw machines screeched and he cut off measured planks, Gus wondered if maybe he had said something Bridger didn't like back at the spring. *Or was it just... our kiss?* Gus obsessed over the possibilities. All that didn't happen, all that could have. However, Gus's biggest distraction throughout his whole day was remembering Bridger's soft, warm lips. All the tingling sensations Bridger gave him still lingered. Gus kept replaying every second of how his best friend had touched him, squeezed him, kissed him.

And then... ran off.

Gus ached to know what had gone wrong. But he also wanted to do it all again.

115

Desperately.

He craved Bridger's scent, that aroma of body spray and natural musk that was still caught in Gus's mind. The sweet taste of Bridger's lips...

Ugh.

Gus put down his sander. He couldn't shake the feeling of Bridger grabbing his waist, pulling him closer, and then pushing him against the workbench. It was electrifying.

The woodshop's phone broke through Gus's brain fog. He perked up and whipped around. Dan set down his tools to answer the call. Gus's breath caught in his throat as his dad chatted with the caller. Gus, hopeful, listened hard. However, as his father mentioned specific furniture costs, Gus's chin fell. He returned to his dull task of sanding the bench before him, crushed.

Why did he even kiss me, then? Why did I kiss him back? I ruined it. I ruined everything.

The full workday passed. Bridger never called.

Saturday morning came without Gus hearing from or seeing Bridger all week. Unwilling to give up, Gus still drove into town to check the skatepark. After locking his dad's Chevy, Gus carried his colorful board toward the sloping bowls. As he approached the mounds, his shaking nerves all came back like it was his first day on this concrete all over again.

Gus's eyes scanned the area for any sign of Bridger, but he only saw a few outskirt members of Max's crew and local rollerblading kids with their parents.

Bridger was nowhere to be found.

Where else could he be?

Undeterred, Gus headed to TJ's down the road, hoping to catch a glimpse of his friend loading up on snacks. No Bridger.

Gus drove through downtown. No Bridger.

Is he angry at me? He wouldn't do anything stupid, would he? Something reckless? Gus shook his head as his eyes rolled up. *It's Bridger. Of course he would.*

Frustrated and anxious, Gus pushed harder on the gas as he sped through town toward Bridger's favorite diner.

At Mark's In & Out, Gus parked in the lot and exited his car. He spotted Tara Shae and her friends sitting outside at a red picnic table for a lunch of burgers, fries, and milkshakes. Gus scoped out the diner in search of Bridger, passing by the girls' laughter and conversation.

"I don't know." Tara folded her arms. "It's been a week, but it was my third interview with them..."

"You have to get it!" Sophia exclaimed. "I bet they don't have any other girls coding for them."

"That's what I'm sayin'," Tara joked as her four friends nodded in agreement.

"When you *do* get it, you better still call me on the weekends," Kelly chimed in, teasing.

"I already promised, didn't I? You girls are what I'll miss most," Tara admitted.

Gus doubled back from the end of the diner, having failed to find Bridger. He walked toward Tara.

"Okay, we'll come visit. But you can't bring your skateboard to the beach if we go to Malibu." Kelly nudged Tara playfully.

"Fine! You know, interestingly, I—"

"Hey, Tara?" Gus interrupted. "Sorry to bother, but have you seen Bridger?"

Tara and all her friends turned to Gus. Some were intrigued, most were confused.

"Oh. Gus! Uh... no, I haven't. Is everything alright?" Tara asked, her brow furrowing.

"Yeah. I. Um. Never mind. Have a good day," Gus replied awkwardly, turning around.

Is he just at home alone? Gus shook his head. *Where else could he be?* An even deeper sense of confusion and worry washed over him.

"Did Bridger do something wrong?" Tara called out.

Gus stopped and turned back around to face her. Tara tilted her head, giving Gus a soft smile.

"If he did, forget about him," she said with a shrug. "You owe him nothing. Don't waste your life sweating over a guy who won't talk to you."

All the girls around her voiced their agreement. They'd all been through this before.

Gus paused. He hadn't thought about it that way.

"Do you want to join us?" Tara offered, gesturing to the table of happy girls.

Gus hesitated, his gaze flickering between Tara and her pals. They seemed fun and comforting, and Gus, wanting support like that, was tempted to sit. Yet his mind was elsewhere. On Bridger.

"Um. No. I've got some... stuff to finish. See you soon though," Gus said.

As Gus turned and walked away from the diner, Tara watched him go. Slightly unsettled, Tara forced herself to shake off the questions that arose and returned to chatting with her friends.

Gus continued his search, exploring different parts of town, hoping to find Bridger.

He drove up to Livingston Park High School.

Nope, he doesn't have summer school on weekends.

Gus passed the lake where, after Bridger pulled him off the dock, they swam together for the very first time. The lake was fully empty.

All that's left is... his house.

Bridger had mentioned where he lived before. It wasn't too far from the skatepark. The boys had skated past it many times, but Bridger never asked Gus to come in. Gus never met his family.

Gus turned onto Bridger's street, only comfortable enough to park a block down the road. He sat nervously behind the wheel. He could see that Bridger's car was in the driveway. He had to be home. There was nowhere else he could be.

Just do it, Gus told himself in his silent car. *Walk up and knock on the door.*

Mid-reach for the car handle, his hand paused. He sighed with meek hesitation.

Him running away? It means he doesn't want to talk to me.

Gus pulled his hand back to his side. He slammed his skull against the headrest behind him, grunting with annoyance. He was stunted by indecision.

If I just tell him that everything's fine, that nothing's wrong, maybe it'll be better. I...

Gus swayed his head back and forth, unsure.

We can forget about the kiss. It doesn't matter. We can go back to how it was before.

He groaned. Even thinking that, he knew it would be impossible. *Fuck! But if I don't try something, he'll forget about me.*

Gus's heart pumped rapidly. His veins filled with adrenaline. *He'll move on if I don't do something. He'll ignore me.*

Gritting his teeth, Gus shoved open the car door and rose from the Chevy. Before he knew it, he was already stomping across the pavement and onto the sidewalk, halfway to Bridger's house.

It's not my fault! We both did this, we both liked it!

Gus stepped onto the Owens family porch. A big white wooden door stood before him.

This year has been terrible enough. I can't lose Bridger too.

Gus knocked on the front door before he could back out. The sound echoed in the quiet neighborhood, and Gus instantly regretted his action. He considered dashing away.

No. We need to talk.

Gus straightened his back and took a deep, nervous breath.

He heard chatter inside the house. Gus immediately wished he was back in his car, that he could drive home. Somehow, he kept his feet planted in place. As footsteps approached the entryway, Gus's stomach soured with nerves. The door pulled back.

"Hello..." A woman with brown hair smiled. Bridger's mom, he figured. "Can I help you?"

"Oh, um. Hi, Mrs. Owens." Gus straightened out anxiously. He fixed his hair. He tried, conspicuously, to peer behind the woman to spot if Bridger was there. "Is... Bridger home?"

"Bridger? No, he's been out all day," his mom answered.

Gus was confused. He had checked everywhere else in town. "Oh, okay. Uh... do you know where he might be?" Gus asked, truly perplexed. "I was hoping to talk with him."

"Probably with Max." The woman shrugged. "Those two are always together."

"Oh. Right," Gus replied, faking a smile. "Maybe I just missed him at the park."

"Yep, he's always skating there. What was your name, sweetie?" Bridger's mom asked.

"I'm Gus. Bridger's friend?"

"Oh? Gus?" Her eyebrows rose with lighthearted confusion. "Bridger's never mentioned you."

The words yanked the hope from Gus as if life's pencil had been ripped away from him. He stepped back slightly, trying not to look as gutted as he felt.

Never... mentioned me?

After exchanging polite but awkward goodbyes, Bridger's mom closed her front door. Gus stood alone on the porch, his head hanging low in defeat.

I'm so stupid.

In the back room of Damage Boardshop, Max and Bridger were furiously playing *Tony Hawk's Underground* on PlayStation 2. Max leaned over and shoved Bridger to mess up his combo. Bridger recoiled, grunted with disbelief, and pushed Max back. The game's timer ran out. Bridger lost.

"Damn it!"

"Yes! Still the king!" Max bellowed with triumph. "No one can beat me!"

Bridger cursed again as he tossed his controller on the couch and rolled his eyes. "I gotta practice more, I guess."

"Nah, you just suck now." Max chuckled, then shook his head. "Too busy hanging with that fairy."

"Who, Gus?"

"Whatever his name is."

"He's not a fairy," Bridger said as he grabbed a controller and started a round of single-player. He thumbed away at the analog sticks, annoyed.

"Seems pretty faggy to me," Max muttered under his breath. His words dripped with disdain.

Bridger stayed silent.

Max turned to glare at Bridger. "Why are you ditching us to hang with him all the time?"

The old friends locked eyes. Bridger's thumbs halted on the controller. Tension sprouted out of nowhere.

"I'm not ditching anyone," Bridger insisted.

"Yeah. You are. What's he got that we don't? He can't even skate," Max argued.

"I don't know why that matters. There's other shit he's good at. He built his own skateboard, taught me how to make my own, his dad's even gonna make more in his—"

"Dude! What the fuck?" Max flew to standing.

Bridger straightened on the couch.

"You think I don't know what this is?" Max pushed before Bridger could say anything.

Bridger's brow started to sweat.

Does he think Gus and I are...

What does he mean?

Fuck...

"This Gus kid hits on Tara, steals my best friend, and now he's trying to put my dad's shop out of business?" Max ranted, starting to pace, clearly upset.

"...Huh?" Bridger looked up.

"I know his dad owns that furniture shop. They better *not* start selling boards," Max threatened.

Bridger laughed in relief. This was... way different than what he expected. "Max, dude, you got it all wrong—"

"You think this is funny?" Max breathed heavily.

"You're acting nuts, bro," Bridger said.

Max stepped closer to his friend. "How long have we known each other?"

"I don't know? A while?"

"A while? How about ten fucking years," Max spat. "And now you're turning your back on me for that fag?"

Bridger avoided Max's gaze.

"Fuck! Why does everyone fuckin' leave?!" Max swatted his beer off the table. Bridger flinched. "I lost my dad. All my friends go off to fucking college. Tara's ignoring me. You! The crew! Even my mom is moving on. The fuck?! I'm doing my best here."

"Max, man. I'm not going anywhere," Bridger assured, trying to calm him down.

Max sighed heavily in frustration. He stared Bridger down.

Bridger didn't like how it felt. *He doesn't own me.*

"You better not," Max whispered, poking Bridger's chest and sitting back down. "We're the same, me and you."

Us? The same? What does he mean?

Things got quiet. Intense. Max was now serious beyond measure.

"Nothing fuckin' breaks us," he said, leaning close to Bridger.

Max went silent. Almost like he wanted to tell Bridger something more...

His eyes searched Bridger's gaze, like an angry wounded dog deciding to trust or attack. He looked down at Bridger's lips, then back up again.

A strange pull had Bridger wanting to move toward Max—that same pull that had brought his lips to Gus's.

But no. This was very different. This was... scary.

"Fuck!" Max backed away from Bridger. He slumped on the lumpy gaming couch and glared up angrily at the skate shop's stained white popcorn ceiling. Max felt trapped beneath it, locked in his own rage prison.

"Why do things always go to shit for me?" Max muttered.

Bridger slowly watched Max, unsettled and confused.

"After my pop died, you went real quiet." Max's voice cut through the tense air.

Bridger hesitated. "But we skated. Every day."

"Well, it wasn't enough."

Bridger gulped, fully lost on what to say.

Gus decided to try the skatepark once again, but Bridger wasn't there. As he walked back to his dad's car, he spotted Tara and her friends chatting at the nearby kid's playground. Sophia was smoking on the bench. Tara and Kelly sat on the swings drinking sodas.

Tara. Gus paused. *She told me to open up.*

Gus walked briskly toward Tara. As he stepped onto the playground grass, the girls turned to him.

"You're not skating?" Tara asked.

Gus said nothing at first, lost in his own mind. Tara realized he was still distracted like the other day and waved him over to have a seat next to her.

"Talk to me. You sure you're okay?" she asked again.

"Yeah," Gus lied, but stepped up next to her. He leaned in toward her swing, away from Kelly.

"Actually, no," he whispered. "Can we talk... privately?"

Tara nodded and looked up at her friend.

"Kelly, can you get me some gum from Sophia? I gotta talk with Gus quick."

Kelly shrugged, grabbed her purse, and went over to the bench with Sophia.

Tara then turned to Gus, waiting for him to speak. They sat in silence as Gus debated how much he wanted to share.

"Bridger and I kissed," Gus slowly revealed.

Tara gasped and slapped his knee, brimming with excitement. "I knew he liked you!"

Gus shook his head. "But something went wrong. He ran off."

"Oh. Hmm." Tara grabbed a lock of her hair and twirled it around her index finger, thinking. "But, I'm glad you told me."

Gus kicked his feet in the sand. "I think he's avoiding me now."

Tara hesitated. "Maybe he's just scared."

Gus's brows knit together. "Scared of what?"

"Losing Max. And you."

They gently swayed in comfortable silence for a moment. Tara spun a slow circle, twisting the chain of her swing.

"When did you know?" Gus eventually asked. "For sure?"

Tara crossed her arms and smiled. "Know what?"

"That you... liked girls."

She let out a soft chuckle, glancing away as she thought.

"When the first Spice Girls album came out." Tara grinned. "I was obsessed. I mean *obsessed*. Posters all over my room, tons of pictures of Mel B. She was *so* hot! At first, I thought I just wanted to be like her. But then I realized I wanted to... well, you know."

Gus thought about his copy of *Thrasher* and nodded, trying not to blush.

Tara gave Gus a head tilt, then let her swing fully untwist, spinning herself around. She dug her feet in the sand to stop and beamed.

"I couldn't tell Sophia or Kelly. They liked the Spice Girls too, but not like me. So I avoided thinking I might like girls by dating guys in high school. Then Max finally asked me out. We'd been close for a while already. He was... actually pretty kind back then. So I said yes."

Gus listened intently as she continued.

"But then someone new transferred to our school. He had painted nails, one earring, and stuck out like a middle finger. Everyone knew he was gay and they bullied him for it, especially Max. One day after class, I asked the guy one question. His response made me know for sure... I was not straight."

Gus stopped swaying, intrigued. "What did you ask?"

"I asked him..." Tara stretched toward Gus, the chains of her swing taut. A knowing glint lit her eyes. "*When did you know you liked boys?*"

Gus gaped at her, realization dawning. He had walked right into that one.

Tara laughed and lifted her feet, letting her swing carry her backward again.

"He gave me this look," she continued, then mimicked it—a look that said, *We're both gay, and you know it.*

Tara held this gaze for a moment before adding, "Sometimes we know our answer. We just need a friend to help us see it."

Gus looked down, his fingers gripping the fabric of his jeans.

"Then! I met this girl named Violet in college. She was a journalism major. We'd stay up talking. *All night*. One study sesh, she kissed me out of the blue and... that was that. I was gay. For sure. I'd never been more certain about anything in my life."

"What happened? After the kiss?" Gus asked.

Tara sighed. "She called it an *experiment*. We never saw each other again."

"Damn. I'm sorry."

"Don't be. She helped me figure myself out."

Gus bounced his knee, lost in thought. "What do you think I should do?"

Tara reached between the swing's chains, placing her hand on Gus's shoulder. "Find Bridger. Talk to him. Tell him how you feel."

The warmth of her hand grounded him.

"Just be honest. That's all *you* can truly control."

"Alright. I'll try." Gus swallowed hard. "You promise not to tell anyone about us?"

"I would never. That's your job." She ruffled his hair affectionately. "Don't worry. You'll figure it out. Tell people, don't tell people. Even I can't tell everyone yet. Max doesn't know about me. But soon, you'll get tired of the secrets. And that's when I finally went, *Fuck it*." She shrugged. "I'd rather be me."

She gave his knee a reassuring pat, then stood up out of her swing.

Gus took a deep breath. He was ready to finally be honest.

But what if Bridger never is?

It was the next day when Gus finally caught Bridger at the skatepark. As he walked toward the concrete, Gus sighed in relief. Bridger stood under the blaring sun, a beacon pulling in a crowd of skater boys. Max and the rest of the crew were watching him do a skate pass.

Gus sat by his tree, deciding to wait to approach when the boys all separated to practice their own runs. It wasn't long before Bridger rounded a corner and spotted Gus on the grass. He swerved sloppily when he caught Gus's eye. Then he kicked up his board and stopped skating.

Gus walked up toward his friend, smiling.

"Hey. How've you been?" Gus greeted.

"Fine," Bridger replied tersely, avoiding Gus's gaze. He checked to ensure the other guys weren't watching him and pulled Gus to the side.

Things were off. Gus felt it. *Uh oh. What do I say?*

"Do you... wanna go work in the woodshop tonight? Or can I skate with you?" Gus asked.

"No, I'm actually hanging with the guys today," Bridger declined distantly.

"Is... something wrong?"

"Gus, I just need time to think. Alone."

"Okay..." Gus replied, shaken. *Why is he talking like this?*

There was a long silence.

Is he mad at me?

"Nothing happened between us," Bridger clarified.

Gus squirmed. Bridger was acting defensive in a way he had never seen before. Gus gulped down new nerves.

"Whatever. It's not a big deal," Gus brushed off.

Bridger took a step back.

Gus's face scrunched up. He forced himself to suppress a new wave of fresh shame.

Bridger could see Gus trying to keep it together. He shifted his weight and looked down.

"I can't..." Bridger struggled to articulate what he wanted to say. "I can't let the guys find out what I... what we... did... okay?"

"What... what does that mean?" Gus asked.

"I can't hang out with you anymore." Bridger stiffened up. "You... should probably go home."

Gus said nothing. *What did I do? I... ugh.* His head fell.

"I'm sorry, Gus," Bridger apologized weakly.

Bridger walked off, leaving Gus confused and abandoned once again.

Gus worked in the woodshop all day that Monday to distract himself. He toiled away on the chairs for a pine table, attempting extreme focus, as his dad finished up the intricate scrollwork behind him. Only by using his hands again to create *something* was Gus able to return to a small sense of normalcy—to what he understood. Keeping active was enough to quiet his brain. After finishing up sawing a flurry of planks to level them and drilling small holes in each, Gus reached to switch out the bit on the drill press. It slipped and clanked to the floor. Gus flinched halfway to picking it up as memories flooded back to him of Bridger dropping this piece the same way back when he first showed him the shop.

No! Gus chided himself. *Stop thinking about Bridger.*

Gus forced his mind to clear and pushed on to the next task. Cleaning up his station, he collected together the scraps of wood beneath his machine and hoisted them into his arms. He turned toward their furnace to burn the scraps. Gus no longer needed them.

Gus inhaled a sharp breath of pain. One of the jagged ends of wood caught the tip of his left hand's ring finger. It drew blood.

Fuck!

Gus dropped the armful of wood. The planks slammed to the ground in a deafening cacophony. A cloud of scattered sawdust burst up around him.

Dan looked up to say something but held his tongue for a moment, sensing Gus's frustration.

"Careful there. You okay? Don't slice a finger off," Dan joked.

"I'm fine," Gus replied curtly.

Dan harrumphed. "Where's Bridger? Haven't seen him around for a while."

"I don't know," Gus replied.

"You guys seemed like good friends," Dan said cautiously.

"Yeah, well. Whatever."

"Something go wrong with making the skateboards?" Dan asked, puzzled.

"No, I—"

Memories of Gus's best and worst moments with Bridger swirled in his brain like a tornado.

The first night meeting under the streetlamps.
Skating together, falling over, laughing.
Building boards in the shop.

Watching the home movies of Mom.
Sleeping so close they could have touched.
The bonfire.
Drawing birds at the lake.
Their fights.
...The kiss.

Gus shook his head to silence it all. He sighed. Gus had no idea how to explain what happened to his father.

He won't get it. Any of it.

"I'm just not someone who can keep his friends," Gus confessed quietly.

Dan's shoulders dropped in worry.

Dejected and stuck in his own head, Gus walked out of the shop to head back to the cabin. Dan stepped forward to follow but stopped himself, unsure of how to help.

Under the evening's amber sky, Bridger skated increasingly fast down a random street far from his house, aimless and upset. He was stressed, distracted. Things had been so different lately—the tense conversation with Max, choosing to cut out Gus, so many of the skate guys still pestering him about getting their homemade skateboards. Bridger didn't know how to deal with so much at once.

Shit... What am I even doing? What did I get myself into?

Skating always cleared Bridger's mind, but he was rarely ever by himself on his board. It was other people that distracted him from his own thoughts. Today, though, Bridger needed time alone.

Bridger floated on his dark flamed skateboard up and down rural roads with the Montana mountains in the far distance. The faster he sped, the more his mind emptied.

Yet an anger remained, and he didn't know why.

I'm an idiot, Bridger badgered himself, skating fast around a bend. *I never asked for this mess.*

Flashbacks of his conversations with Gus at the bonfire and at the secret lake came to him.

Why did I tell him all those things?

Bridger shook his head violently to shoo the memories away. He winced with heavy regret and kicked off to skate even faster. Soon Bridger approached a steep downward hill. And of all things, he smiled.

Perfect. Bridger spread his wingspan wide and closed his eyes. *Here we go.*

Bridger careened down the hill, basking in the familiar rush of the wind zipping by his face. The airy, dangerous freedom of going so fast. Of flying. *This* danger felt normal to him. The adrenaline was better than guilt, better than confusion. He craved it. Relished it. He Swooped his arms like one of Gus's birds.

Gus would hate this.

A haze of memories descended over Bridger's mind. Moments of touch, the almost-kiss, that first electrifying make-out...

But Max's angry words broke through.

"We're the same, me and you."

NO! FUCK YOU! Bridger jerked to the side to escape the memory, to escape what Max thought he knew about him. *We're NOT the same!*

Gus's calming face appeared back in his mind, but it was too late. Bridger swerved, wobbled, and fell hard off his board. He rolled a few paces down the hill. The flesh of his right arm ripped as he scraped the rocky road.

Bridger yelped. *Fuck! Shit!*

On the ground, Bridger gritted his teeth against the pain. He inspected the damage. A large scrape up his arm's side leaked blood down to his elbow.

He cursed angrily, clutching his bloody arm, and kicked his board away.

The skateboard rolled far from him as he sat—broken, tired, and ashamed—on the ground.

After leaving the woodshop and ending his distracted workday, Gus entered his bedroom and slinked onto his mattress, teary-eyed and full of regret. His whole body was sore. He stewed there, wishing he could melt into his bed. Gus grunted and turned onto his side. This whole summer had become a waste of time. He hadn't practiced his sketching in days, he'd saved up barely any money for college from working with Dad, he'd spent so much time learning to skateboard for a friendship he didn't even have anymore.

I'm not myself. Bridger distracted me.

I gotta move on.

Gus sighed.

But... I miss him.

Just last week, Gus was flying higher than his favorite sparrows. He'd had it all. He and Bridger had worked so hard. On his skating lessons, on their carpentry, on their friendship...

Were we actually friends? More than that?

Was he just using me?

Gus thought he had built something really special with Bridger—whatever it was. Bridger made him happy. He hated that Bridger now consumed his every thought.

But at the same time, Gus loved it.

Bridger had unlocked in Gus new passions he never knew he could love. He came to Montana with no plan and nothing to do. Bridger helped this summer make sense. Without him, that sense was evaporating, leaving Gus feeling as lost and isolated as when he arrived. He loathed that feeling of moving backward, of not knowing his next step. *What's happening to me?*

For the first time in his life, Gus felt terrified of a blank page.

I wish Mom were here.

Gus smiled morosely, remembering all the late-night advice his mother would always give him, even when he didn't ask. School bullies, challenging classes, failed art projects—his mom's sage words and warm hugs had soothed them all.

She'd know what to do.

Gus's nose twitched. His eyes started burning. He felt slow tears starting to flow. A renewed grief hit Gus, punching through the emptiness left from losing Bridger, a loss so raw and new that it ripped open a deeper wound.

I'll never get to hug her again.

She'll never see the art I make.

She'll never meet my first... boyfriend.

Alone in his room, Gus wept. He couldn't hold back as his cramping stomach pulled him into a cradled ball of heartache. Waves of sadness flowed through him. He couldn't stop sobbing. Couldn't stop thinking about all his tiny cherished dreams for their future Mom had taken with her.

Gus wiped a fresh wave of tears and his gaze fell upon his sketchbook lying on the locked wooden trunk by his bed. The sketchbook he hadn't touched since kissing Bridger. The sketchbook his mom gave him last year before she got sick...

If I don't have her, why am I even drawing anymore?

With a vicious, callous grunt, Gus began tearing out all his work page by page. Each and every stunning sketch was ripped from the book's spine by hands trembling with anger and disappointment and hurt. He didn't want these memories anymore. He wanted the regrets to stop. Minnesotan loons in clear lakes—*torn in half.* The blue jays amongst the flowers behind his grandparents' house—*crumpled into balls.* Every eclectic object in his mother's Minnesota apartment—*ripped into scraps.*

Gus scooped up the first pile of torn paper and dumped it into the wastebasket at his feet. He grabbed his sketchbook and continued again, unable to stop. As Minnesota drawings transitioned to depictions of Montana, Gus's sense of loss morphed into bitter betrayal.

If Bridger doesn't want me, I don't want Montana.

Gus ripped out the pristine mountains he'd sketched as his dad drove him from the airport, and tore them down the middle. He furiously shredded all the stupid pages of various skater boys and their boards. The baby sparrow stuck on the ground with its broken wing, he shredded without a care. Gus wanted them all gone.

His fingers paused with the last drawing he found: a golden Bridger sunbathing in their secret spot. Gus had drawn every muscle on Bridger's torso as he lay on the rock above the spring—had captured every water droplet streaming down his drying legs. It had been Gus's final sketch right before his and Bridger's muddy escape in the rain, their first passionate kisses.

Gus hesitated. He strained against the heated pain. His face scrunched up with depressed confusion, and tears welled anew. Staring into the sketched eyes of the beautiful Bridger, Gus lost himself once more in that golden moment. He craved the safety he'd thought they shared. He had taken it for granted, how close he and Bridger had come, not knowing it could all crumble so fast.

I'm not letting anyone get that close again. No one.

Gus's wet sullen eyes fell to a dead stare as he slowly ripped Bridger's sketch right through his sun-kissed chest. With scorched ambivalence, Gus dumped the two halves of Bridger into the trash can on the ground with all the rest of his memories.

It was done. All his pages were gone. No going back.

Gus chucked the empty sketchbook on top of it all.

One loose paper he'd missed slipped out, torn halfway from the binding. Gus grimaced and reached down to rip it in half. It stuck to the front cover; he pried it away.

Smiling up at him from the page, sitting on the porch of their Minnesota home, was his mother. Gorgeous, serene, and happy.

Gus clutched this last sketch he'd drawn of her in his fist. The world stopped. His hand relaxed. In a panic, he smoothed it back out, wiping away the creases of damage he had done.

No. Not this one.

When he lowered back onto his bed, gently cradling the sketch of his mother close to his chest, Gus found he had no tears left to cry. Numb, he reached for his headphones and played metal so loud he couldn't possibly think.

She's gone, too.

No more Mom. No more Bridger.

Gus lay there, his music a racket, feeling as torn, discarded, and useless as the scraps in his trash.

From Drowning to Mountaintops

A few days later, when the summer sun was almost too bright, Bridger drove toward Bozeman to go swimming at Rocky Creek with Bennet, Avery, and Coop—his oldest friends. While Max and Gus had taken up most of Bridger's time recently, Avery, Bennet, and Coop had been Bridger's best boys since preschool.

All four teenagers dashed to the center of the rusty rural bridge over Rocky Creek's swimming hole, shed their street clothes, and cannonballed into the water below.

Laughter echoed along the creek and nearby forest as the friends swam, splashed, and dunked each other in the water.

"These last couple of weeks, we've barely seen you," Avery remarked, splashing Bridger.

"Yeah, I almost forgot what your face looked like," Bennet chimed in.

The four boys all treaded water as they shot the shit. Even this far out of town, their quick conversations always returned to skateboarding.

"Skating's been rough," Coop said. "Max showing off sucks without you there to make us laugh about it."

"I've been busy," Bridger replied, not wanting to share more.

"Making skateboards with Gus?" Avery pressed, curiosity piqued.

"I guess, yeah. But it was too much work," Bridger explained. "I just need a break."

"It'll be worth it for those badass boards he's making us," Avery responded. "That's still happening, right?

Bridger nodded, but he didn't even truly know that answer himself.

"Isn't Gus sorta a nerd?" Coop ventured.

Avery shrugged. "He's chill, I like him."

"I heard he's gay," Bennet added.

The world stopped. Bridger forgot to tread water and slipped under for a second. Recovered. *Shit.*

"He *is* a bit..." Coop said before limping his wrist.

Who's saying that about Gus? Shit.

The other boys' nonchalant voices distorted in Bridger's ears as he struggled to play it cool, terrified of *that* word being brought up by any of his friends.

"It's not a rumor if only Max thinks so. Max calls everything gay," Avery joked casually.

"Gus is leaving soon, right?" Coop asked, turning to Bridger.

However, Bridger was fully out of it, not paying attention, still worried about the boys even mentioning *Gus* and *gay*. Two thoughts he was currently trying to avoid.

"Bridger? ...Hello?" Coop leaned in.

The other boys, quizzical, all looked over.

"Earth to Bridger!" Avery splashed him.

Bridger snapped out of his haze. "What?"

"Your friend Gus is leaving for some fancy college soon, right?" Coop inquired.

"He's not really my friend," Bridger replied distantly. "But yeah, he's going to Rhode Island."

"Good for him. I'm stuck here forever," Avery lamented.

"Yeah. I almost flunked last year." Bennet laughed. "I'm not going anywhere important."

Bridger shook his head with annoyance. "Who cares about college?! I don't wanna think about anything past this summer. I just wanna chill with you guys. No more distractions!"

The three friends exchanged puzzled looks.

"Distractions?" Bennet spoke up.

"Did something more happen with Sophia since the bonfire?" Avery prodded.

"Or did she think your dick was too small and dump you?" Coop teased.

The boys all laughed.

Oh, right. Sophia. Shit.

Bridger feigned a boastful nonchalance to play along. "Nah, I'm too much man for Sophia," he retorted with a grin. The others all scoffed.

"Yeah, right!"

"My ass!"

"Fine. Sure. Sophia fizzled out." Bridger chuckled, back to feeling normal.

"Makes sense. She's too hot for us, just like all of Tara's friends."

"Yeah, we can only get medium-level chicks."

"Speak for yourselves. Rachel and I are still fuckin'," Coop boasted, prompting eye rolls.

"Exactly. Medium-level chicks," Bridger joked.

All the guys laughed at Coop and ganged up to splash him. Bridger smiled, feeling comfortable. Too comfortable.

"Besides, I'm into someone new," Bridger let slip.

Immediately, his friends pounced on him for more information.

"Really?! Who? Kelly?"

Fuck!

"Kiana?"

"Trish? That girl that works at the diner?"

"I don't want to talk about it," Bridger deflected, waving them away.

"You brought it up!" Coop shouted in jest.

"I hear Max is planning a rager for his birthday in a week or so," Bridger interjected.

Avery laughed. "Dude, don't change the subject!"

"Who's the girl?" Coop pressed on.

"Stephanie? Jess? Beth from math class?" Bennet listed off. "I can go all day."

The boys moved closer, surrounding Bridger so he couldn't escape.

Fuck. I can't tell them anything, Bridger fretted. *They'll blab all around town.*

"I'm not saying who! Fuck off!" Bridger said, defensive again.

"Why?" Bennet shrugged. "She ugly?"

Bridger laughed uncomfortably as all the guys stared at him, not letting up. He didn't know what to say. *Fuck!*

Frantically wanting to escape, Bridger dropped beneath the river's surface. He held his breath under the water, opened his eyes, and saw the wavy, undulating forms of his friends still pestering him to name his *girl.*

Cooper laughed from above. "That's it. She must be an uggo."

"Maybe she's one of Max's ex-hookups?" Avery suggested. "He'd keep that a secret."

Coop scoffed. "He's just being a wuss."

"We'll get it eventually," Bennet assured them.

Bridger still couldn't ignore all their digs, not even underneath the water.

I'm such an idiot.

Bridger felt like crying and screaming all at once. He had no way out. He wanted to stay submerged and never go back up. His lungs burned, but Bridger didn't care. He'd rather drown right here in the river than let his friends know he—that he—

Fuck! Bridger cursed down with the minnows. *Fuck them, man. They're not getting shit out of me.*

"Bridger?" Avery waved at him through the water's barrier, "Come back up, man."

"Yeah, dude." Bennet sounded worried. "It's been a long time."

"Quit being dramatic, man," Coop piled on.

The three boys exchanged curious, puzzled expressions. Bridger had never acted like this around them before.

Bridger was lost on what to do. *They're never gonna give up now.* Bridger's whole chest threatened to collapse. *If they find out I... that I... like Gus. It's all over.*

His throat started closing in on itself. But Bridger would rather die right here than look like an idiot in front of the guys.

They can't know. I'll never live it down. They'll tell everyone.

"Dude! Come up," Avery called to him. "Quit joking."

Bennet fell into a panic. "He's gonna drown down there."

"I'm pullin' him out." Coop grabbed Bridger's arm and yanked.

Bridger resisted. He planted his feet in the rocky sand and leaned back with all his weight. *I'm not gonna let them make fun of me.* His lips were turning blue. There was a weird pain in his right eye.

"Bridger?! What the fuck!" Coop called out when he failed to pull Bridger up. "Guys, help me!"

All three of Bridger's oldest friends grabbed his arm in a morbid game of tug-of-war, struggling to tow him above the surface.

A sleepy lightheadedness overcame Bridger. It was... nice.

"PULL HARDER!"

Avery?

For a second, Bridger closed his eyes.

With a splash and three loud grunts, the boys lifted their friend with their combined strength back above the river's surface. The three friends immediately cursed at Bridger as he flailed and coughed and swallowed water in all the commotion. He immediately hacked up the liquid that hit his throat and took a deep breath, finally letting fresh oxygen re-enter his lungs.

Bridger wished he were still drowning.

"Dude! Are you psychotic?!" Coop berated him.

"Bridger, that was not cool," Bennet complained.

The guys all backed away from Bridger to give him some space.

"Then just leave me the fuck alone!" Bridger blurted out. "Stop asking me questions."

Silence fell amongst the four in the river. All that remained was the buzz of cicadas and the rustle of trees from the light wind.

"Dude, we don't *actually* care who you're crushing on," Avery softened. "Calm down."

"Yeah right." Bridger, still angry, didn't believe him.

"Well, it's not worth you doing *that*..." Avery breathed.

"Yeah, man. It's whatever. We're all friends here." Coop shrugged. "Girls can't get between us."

"Even if she's Beth from math class," Bennet joked, trying to lighten the mood.

Bridger paused. His heart beat so fast that he had to gasp again for air. It was this, or perhaps his frustration, that made the words spill out before he could even catch himself.

"What if it's not a girl?"

Bennet scratched his head. Coop and Avery locked eyes. Then their mouths fell open slowly. The boys all waded forward again.

"What do you mean?" Avery grilled Bridger.

"Like a g-guy?" Coop choked.

"I... I don't know." Bridger started to shut down again.

"Yes you do," Avery countered.

"Promise you won't tell!" Bridger got a bit aggressive, raising his voice. "Not anyone!"

Avery splashed backward. "Dude, quit freakin' me out."

"We'll keep it locked up."

Bennet nodded. "Just you and us."

Bridger closed his eyes, then took a long, deep sigh. He could not believe he was even considering telling them. *These idiots are going to ruin my life.* But...

The lying, the secrets... It was all becoming too hard. Bridger was tired. He couldn't take it anymore.

"I may have... had a thing. A weird moment," Bridger shared softly.

Bennet shook his head. "I'm confused."

"With a guy?" Avery pressed. "Which guy?"

"I didn't say a guy," Bridger evaded.

"Is it Gus?" Coop said what everyone was thinking.

"No!" *Shit!* It was all happening too fast for him. "I mean, we..."

Avery's eyes widened and he punched Bennet beside him. "It IS Gus!"

"Woah." Bennet rubbed his sore arm, mouth agape.

"You're GAY?!" Coop exclaimed.

Bridger's stomach fell to his feet. He should have just drowned. He could not handle this.

I gotta get out of here. Now.

"I'm leaving," Bridger declared.

Embarrassed and angry at himself, Bridger turned to swim toward shore. He'd only made it a few strokes before his friends cornered him again.

"Bridger, stop!" Avery called out.

"Dude! Don't leave," Coop yelled.

Bridger turned around, dead with his emotions. He braced for more jokes, more taunting. For worse. He glared at each of them.

"Quit running away," Coop stated. "We don't care if you're gay."

"Yeah. Gus is cool." Avery shrugged his agreement.

"I just want my skateboard," Bennet chimed in.

"Shut up, Bennet!" Avery splashed him.

The three boys went silent, waiting for Bridger to speak. They had weirdly calm expressions on their faces that Bridger struggled to understand. They were being *nice* to him. They genuinely wanted to know how he was feeling.

"So," Coop broke the silence, "you like guys?"

"I mean, I still like girls..." Bridger admitted, his voice shaky. "I just also... like Gus."

"Wow," Coop breathed.

"Okay." Avery nodded. "Cool."

Bennet pumped his fist. "More girls for me."

Coop shoved Bennet and burst out laughing. "Fat chance!"

"*Better* chance at least!" Bennet gestured at Bridger.

Bridger watched his friends, his eyes wide. They were still acting like the same old idiots. They weren't even laughing at him, but at each other.

They don't care...

Bridger smiled.

"So, what happened with Gus?" Avery inquired.

"Did you hook up?" Coop asked.

"No! We made out sorta." Bridger turned red. "We also almost kissed this other time."

"That's it?!"

"Lame!"

"I don't know." Bridger wiped water from his face. "I do like him, but I think I may have screwed it up."

"How?" Avery pressed.

Bridger sighed. "Running away."

Coop shook his head. "Stupid."

"Hey!" Bridger retorted.

"Well, shit, at least you have someone." Bennet smacked the water. "I can't get *any* girl to look my way."

"Yeah. Go fix it, B," Coop nudged. "Or you'll be a virgin like Bennet forever!"

"Hey!" Bennet protested. He and Coop started a splash fight.

As Coop and Bennet floated off, ruthlessly trying to dunk each other, Avery stayed quiet by Bridger's side. Avery nodded slowly at his best friend and put his arm on his shoulder.

"Thanks for telling us, Bridge." Avery smiled. "I know it must have been hard."

Bridger felt his eyes start to moisten. He fought back the tears and nodded with a quivering lip.

"It was," Bridger slowly confirmed, the only thing he could say in response.

"Well, don't worry." Avery squeezed his shoulder and smiled. "We got your back, dude."

A wave of relief rushed over Bridger, this sense of freedom that he had never felt in his entire life.

"Just go talk to Gus," Avery suggested gently. Then he nodded at Cooper and Bennet, still roughhousing in the background. "And finish up our boards already, yeah?"

Bridger snorted. Avery smirked. The longtime friends shared a smile.

"Yeah. Yeah, maybe I'll do that," Bridger responded.

Avery fist-bumped Bridger and swam off to join in dunking Bennet. Bridger shook his head with disbelief as the weight of what just happened left his body. He chuckled to himself. He never felt more grateful for these bozos than he did right now.

Gus lay alone in his bedroom, zoned out, staring at his ceiling. He was baking in the sweltering attic. It was his day off, and he had nothing to do. His skateboard sat unused in the corner. He no longer had a sketchbook to draw in. All he wanted to do was move on with his life and start college in a new state.

Maybe, over there, things will finally work out for me. Maybe, for once, I won't screw everything up.

Footsteps barged into Gus's room and a backpack landed on his stomach with a painful *thump.*

"What the—"

"Get up. We're going for a hike," Dan announced from the doorway.

"What? Why? I don't want to," Gus protested.

"Too bad. No more moping around," Dan stated. "I'm getting you out of this funk."

Gus groaned, propping himself up on his elbows. "Do I really have to?"

"Yes. We've both been invited," Dan said.

"Invited?" Gus asked, confused. "By who?"

Dan pointed downstairs. "Go check outside."

Perplexed but intrigued, Gus swung his legs over the side of his bed, stood up, and made his way out of his room, passing his father without a word.

About to close Gus's door, something caught Dan's attention. On the bedroom wall hung an image he hadn't seen in years but recognized instantly. His wife's bitterroot flower painting. He stepped back into the room to get a better look at it, recalling too many lost memories. He shook his head and moved backward. His heel hit something.

Peering down, Dan's gaze fell upon a tipped-over trash can. He reached to fix it and saw, discarded and torn up inside it, his son's sketchbook.

Dan slowly sat on Gus's bed and lifted the trash can to his lap, pulling out the shredded book. His shoulders dropped with gloom.

He sifted through all the torn scraps of Gus's Minnesota nature sketches and of his last two months in Montana. Seeing the minute details of black-and-white scenes he hadn't lived, Dan realized this sketchbook hid a whole secret life Gus never shared with him. He released a deep sigh of sorrow.

Dan fished out a few ripped strips of paper and, putting them together, connected the puzzle pieces of Bridger's young face. His gaze lifted to the cabin window. Shaking his graying head and closing his tired eyes, his mind filled with freshly rooted regrets.

As Gus made it to their cabin's mudroom, he opened the front door and was taken aback to find Bridger standing there. The sight of him after not seeing his friend for days sent Gus's stomach spinning.

"Hey." Bridger said softly.

Gus stayed silent.

"I made a mistake." Bridger's face was mournful as he looked up at Gus from the cabin's front steps.

"About what?" Gus asked, slow to show any sort of reaction.

"Ditching you. I was a bad friend," Bridger confessed.

"So now you want to... hike?" Gus was unsure of what Bridger's sudden appearance was supposed to mean. He was reluctant to even be standing here, risking something else bad happening. He just wanted to go back to his room and be alone.

"Your dad said you needed cheering up," Bridger explained. "And I know why..."

Bridger's gaze, full of sincerity, met Gus's. Gus searched between Bridger's oddly shy eyes for meaning. He was still confused and hurt, but Gus couldn't help but deflate slightly. A small smile touched his lips.

Dan drove both Gus and Bridger far from his property in the red 1969 Chevy up to the base of Mount Blackmore. Bridger and Dan had both hiked Blackmore Trail and seen Hyalite Lake before, but it was Gus's first time. Bridger dashed up the trail as Gus and Dan followed behind, all of them enjoying the lush scenic views. Bridger started picking up the rarer off-colored stones and placing them in his pocket. He threw one as far as he could. A flock of fluttering sparrows abandoned some trees in the distance, squawking in protest.

"Oops! I scared your bird friends." Bridger winked at Gus.

Gus reluctantly smiled, rolling his eyes, but still took a few strides to catch up to Bridger. Dan let the boys climb ahead as they continued hiking.

Eventually, Dan found a rocky clearing where they could stop to cook dinner. All three dropped their bags. As Dan pulled out some supplies, Bridger leaned down and plucked free a small wildflower. He admired the tiny blossom for a moment, loving how exquisite it was up close. Bridger then held it out to a surprised Gus.

"Here. Bring this home and draw it for me." Bridger smiled gently, catching Gus's gaze.

"Really?" Gus asked, suspicious of all this behavior. He tossed a glance his dad's way, but the man was laser-focused on the supplies.

"Yeah." Bridger's hand reached to confidently tuck the flower behind Gus's ear. "I wanna see how it looks through your eyes."

Gus blushed. Bridger never spoke to him this way. It was strange and new.

Gus liked it.

"Gus, can you get us some firewood?" Dan asked his son without looking up.

"Yeah," Gus replied as casually as he could manage.

"Can I come with?" Bridger offered.

"Sure. I guess," Gus responded, still wary of Bridger.

The boys headed off together toward the nearby wood as Dan organized the food he had brought from the cabin. They weaved through the forest's lodgepole pines and quaking aspen trees, scanning for small dry logs to pick up. They weren't speaking. The burbling creek, trilling bugs, and calling birds filled the air around them. Occasionally, one of the boys would lean down when they found a suitable broken branch on the ground for kindling.

Bridger was contemplating whether he should break the quiet to say something. He stopped walking and stood still. Gus looked over.

Bridger took a deep breath and started playing with one of his sticks, hitting it against the ground. "I'm just gonna say it. I'm sorry."

"Sorry for what?" Gus tried to keep a blank face. "Nothing happened."

Bridger looked down at the forest floor, regretting using those specific words last week, but forced himself to push forward.

"I... messed up," Bridger said. "I shouldn't have ignored you."

Gus stayed quiet. He turned away from Bridger to keep walking. He picked up a new piece of wood. *What is all of this? The flower? This hike?* He needed to know.

"Why did you ignore me?" Gus asked without turning around. "To go from hanging out every day to... to nothing? Did I do something wrong?"

"No. It wasn't you. It was me." Bridger followed slowly behind.

"I *liked* what happened," Gus revealed, his words firm even though he couldn't bring himself to look back at Bridger.

Bridger smiled to himself behind Gus as he walked in tandem with his stride along the streaming creek.

"Me too," Bridger finally admitted, almost in a whisper.

Now Gus did turn around. One eyebrow lifted. "You did?"

"Yeah. I liked it... almost too much." Bridger smirked slyly, gazing up at Gus.

And all Gus could do was laugh. "Then why'd you run away, you idiot?!"

A chuckle burst free from Bridger. The tension evaporated. Bridger took a deep breath, tapping his stick again with nerves on the brink of excitement.

"I just got scared, Gus. Okay?" he said. "It all happened so fast."

Gus nodded. He lifted his shoulders in thought. "I know we...

did something new, but... I never planned any of this." Gus shrugged. "I don't know how to do it right."

"Me neither." Bridger chortled. "It was definitely... new."

Bridger took a slow step toward Gus. They were a few yards apart.

"When I'm with the other guys," Bridger pondered aloud, "I feel like I have to impress them. All the time. I never get to relax."

Bridger adjusted the firewood in his arms clumsily. He took another step.

"When I'm near girls, it's like they're pretty aliens," he continued. "I have no idea what to say."

The boy seemed so nervous. Gus's chest warmed as Bridger inched even nearer. If he got any closer, Gus would lose his mind.

He wanted to lose his mind.

"But with you, I can just... *breathe*," Bridger softly admitted. "I'm not used to that."

Gus nodded cautiously, shakily, and kept listening.

Bridger laid the firewood down on the ground, then stood back up.

Gus's eyebrows rose. Bridger was a foot away. He could reach out and touch Gus if he wanted to.

Please want to.

"It's only been two months, but being around you has made me rethink some things. Want to try *new* things," Bridger confided.

Gus, desperate and bold, took a step toward Bridger. "Try what?" he asked.

"Being... more than friends," Bridger whispered.

Gus's heartbeat couldn't help but quicken. His eyes darted back and forth. He and Bridger were only inches apart.

Bridger leaned in and kissed Gus.

Gus dropped his firewood to the forest floor as his eyes melted shut. Bridger put his hand softly on the back of Gus's neck as they connected, pulling him in. A flurry of magnetic energy enveloped the boys as they squeezed each other tighter and kissed deeper. It felt natural, full, exhilarating.

Both boys slowly pulled apart. Bridger looked at Gus's rosy

pink face for a reaction.

Gus smiled, which made Bridger smile.

"I... um... I like you, Gus," Bridger finally said aloud. "A lot."

"I really like you, too," Gus comforted.

The boys picked up their firewood and carried the heavy piles back through the forest to Dan at the campsite. Gus's father was cutting up some vegetables and casually nodded to both boys as they dropped off the kindling. Together, all three worked to build a fire. Dan roasted some spicy marinated chicken legs on a metal grate over the flames with some halved onions and sweet potatoes.

The trio sat on big rocks around the fire pit as the delicious aromas of the cooking food mixed with the sweet smell of smoked pine. Bridger shared funny childhood stories of adventures on these hills with Avery, Coop, and Bennet, making Gus laugh and even Dan crack a grin. Every time Gus's father had to poke the fire or turn to grab something from his bag, Bridger and Gus snuck in thrillingly flirty smiles and lingering looks. Both knew they'd be kissing a lot more very soon.

With the meal finished and the conversations fading, Dan and the boys sat in the glowing smoky silence to soak in the fire's warm comfort. Dusk was approaching. Soon they would need to head back down the mountain. Before it got dark. But for now, they all knew the value of enjoying this gift of peace and quiet together. Eventually, of all people, Gus's father was the first to break the tranquility.

"You know..." Dan shared a rare smile. "I haven't had a day off like this in a long, long time."

Chapter 13

Max's Party

The next week was a rapid technicolor daydream Gus could never have pictured outside his sketchbook. Gus and Bridger indulged in all their favorite activities around town, just now with increasing intimacy. When Bridger first yanked Gus into Livingston Lake weeks ago, they were alone. Now local families were here and kids were swimming all around. The boys still roughhoused and splashed in the water. But this time, Bridger also kept attempting to steal hidden kisses from Gus under the lake's surface. At a crowded Mark's In & Out, the boys smirked at each other while sharing french fries and pepper ketchup for dinner because *only they knew* they were on a secret late-night date in plain sight beneath the glowing neon BEEF-BURGERS sign. They let their knees touch under the table and snuck each other lewd winks, plotting to make out later in private.

At the skatepark, Gus started practicing with Tara and chatted with her friends while Bridger rode with Max and his crew on the park's other side. Coop, Avery, and Bennet jostled Bridger with sly swipes and noogies every time he checked on Gus in the distance, proud to see their friend had properly fixed his mistakes.

Since Bridger would visit Gus's cabin more and more for clandestine make-outs and innocent sleepovers, Dan reluctantly allowed Bridger to help them with small tasks in the woodshop. Dan was surprised at how quickly Bridger adapted to his instructions and eventually trusted the boy with more work; likewise, Gus was surprised by every stealthy slap to his butt Bridger delivered unbeknownst to Dan.

Gus could never have drawn a picture colorful enough to capture this first week of falling in love with Bridger.

After a few successfully smooth days of woodworking together, Dan agreed to help the boys complete their skateboard orders for Coop, Bennet, and Avery. The middle-aged man polished off the layered, shaped plies of the three wooden boards, Gus painted the requested deck designs, and Bridger attached the baseplates, trucks, and wheels with a practiced ease that came from exchanging the hardware on his own decks over the years. Once all three of their first *SCRAPS* board orders were finished, Gus and Bridger were buzzing to deliver their first products to their first loyal clients.

The boys drove to McNair, parked the Chevy, and ran up to the concrete edge of the skatepark to see Coop, Bennet, and Avery already riding the bowls and shooting the shit at the other end.

"Yo! Guys! Get over here!" Bridger called out to them.

The three all looked up while weaving in between each other, slowed down, and popped up their boards.

"What?!" Coop screamed back.

"DELIVERY!" Bridger held two new boards up in the air. Gus belatedly held up the third. The two shared a look of pride as their first customers whooped with joy across the park.

The three skaters kicked off again, speeding through the small, sloping concrete mounds to swipe their new decks from Gus and Bridger as they zoomed by them.

The boys smoothed to a stop.

"Bro! This is epic!" Avery inspected the hand-painted heavy metal bass guitar, lightning, and screeching music notes on his deck.

"Gus, you are a beast!"

"Yeah! Shit, Gus! This wolf looks real!" Coop's fingers grazed his board's layered acrylic painting of a howling wolf under a midnight moon. He turned to dab up a startled Gus.

"For a gay guy, you still gave this milf some nice knockers!" Bennet joked, giving the back of his skateboard a sloppy wet kiss.

"Bennet!" Bridger shoved him to shut up as Gus chuckled and looked at his toes.

"Can we test 'em?" Avery asked Gus and Bridger.

Bridger looked to Gus, who nodded. Bridger gestured out to the park in front of them, grinning proudly. "Knock yourselves out."

Coop, Bennet, and Avery immediately jumped onto their new boards and shot down the concrete, dispersing to the various portions of the skatepark. Coop did a flip at the top of a quarter pipe, Avery rode the flat bar, and Bennet went around and around one bowl in circles.

Soon the boys skated back to Gus and Bridger, kicking up their boards and holding them tight.

"Bridge." Avery chuckled. "It's like skatin' on butter."

"Yeah. So smooth," Coop agreed. "And it didn't feel like it was gonna snap right under me when I got air."

Bennet shook his head. "I can't go back to my one now."

"That's what we like to hear." Bridger smirked toward Gus, then held his hand out to his friends. "That'll be $150 each, boys."

The friends all laughed. Coop, Bennet, and Avery pulled out wads of crumpled cash from their pockets, having come prepared.

"Max's birthday rager's this weekend. We're all going right?" Bennet asked the group.

Bridger turned to Gus. Both looked unsure.

"College girls and lots of booze?" Coop nodded with excitement. "Of course."

Avery laughed. "Yeah, plus it's Max. He'll kill me if I miss it."

Bridger sighed. "I want to go, but not without Gus."

"And Max still doesn't like me," Gus reminded them all.

"So probably not." Bridger shrugged to his friends.

"C'mon!" Bennet complained. "You can't *not* go, B. Max will wanna drink with you."

"Gus, you should come. Just be where Max isn't," Coop suggested. "Sneak him in, Bridger."

Avery gave them a knowing look. "Could be the perfect place to sell some boards…"

Bridger and Gus locked eyes with raised eyebrows. They both nodded.

Saturday night, Bridger drove Gus to a large house on the outskirts of Livingston. Gus told Bridger that this wasn't Max's house, which would have been too small for his party. The place belonged to one of Max's older friends, on break from Missoula College. His parents were out of town.

Blaring music and flickering strobe lights beckoned from inside as the boys walked up to the house from Bridger's parked car. Under their arms were their skateboards. They hoped people here would ask about their deck designs so they could nab some sales. And there were *a lot* of people here. Crowds of kids their age and older were already drinking, even on the front porch. Gus gulped. He didn't know why, but a wave of anxiety crashed over him.

Inside, they navigated through a sea of people until they finally spotted Coop, Bennet, and Avery amidst the crowd.

"Where's the Birthday Boy?" Bridger called out over the music.

"About six beers down in the back," Coop replied, gesturing with his red plastic cup.

Bridger tapped Gus. "I'll be right back." They shared a smile, then Bridger veered off with Coop, Bennet, and Avery to go find Max.

"Gus!"

Gus turned and found himself grinning as Tara approached him from across the room. Her presence amidst the chaos immediately calmed his nerves. "Tara! Hi."

"Hey. I heard a rumor you're making more boards," she remarked.

Gus nodded eagerly, lifting his board as proof of merchandise. He also retrieved a crumpled flyer from his pocket to show her. "We're trying to convince my dad to actually sell them in his shop. Would you maybe wanna buy one?" he proposed with a small grin.

Tara examined the sample designs and price ranges on the flyer and smirked. "Yeah, duh!"

Gus's face lit up.

Bridger and his boys returned as Gus and Tara were enthusiastically discussing her board ideas.

"We can't find Max anywhere," Avery announced.

"He's probably taking a leak," Coop quipped.

Bennet jolted to a stop when he saw Tara standing with Gus. "Oh! Hi. Hello. Tara..."

Tara didn't even see him. Gus could hear Coop comment to Bennet, "You're so lame, dude."

Bridger slipped in behind Gus to whisper into his ear.

"Meet me on the roof," he breathed.

Goosebumps covered Gus's neck as Bridger's lips grazed his ear. He watched as Bridger shuffled away and traveled up a nearby staircase. Before turning the flight's corner, Bridger shot Gus a steamy gaze, then disappeared to the second floor.

"And what was *that*?" Tara placed a hand on Gus's shoulder, pulling back his attention.

Gus blushed. "Nothing!"

"Gus! I saw that look from Bridger!" she exclaimed in a hushed eager whisper. "Did something more happen between you two?"

Gus beamed at Tara and hurried off.

Tara's mouth dropped open behind him and her eyes glowed with pride. She raised her drink to Gus as he dashed up the steps.

Upstairs, Gus walked through a dark second-floor hallway with various sounds coming out of closed-door rooms with god-knows-what happening inside. At the very end of the corridor, a dull yellow light issued from behind a partly open bedroom door.

"Bridger?"

Gus gently pushed the door open. The homemade board he'd built for Bridger leaned against the far wall. Above it was an open double-paned window. Its short white curtain billowed in the night's gentle breeze. He peeked over the window's ledge and saw the familiar backside of the beguiling boy sitting on the lower roof by himself.

Gus smiled. He placed his own skateboard against the wall next to Bridger's.

Carefully climbing out the window, Gus brightened as Bridger turned to see him step onto the short roof. Bridger reclined back on the shingles beneath the starry night sky, his smile gentle and warm.

"Hey," Gus greeted slowly as he settled down beside Bridger.

"Hey," Bridger responded.

Downstairs at the party, a tipsy Max exited the first-floor bathroom and stumbled his way back to his friends near the pseudo dance floor in the living room, weaving through beer-sipping college students.

"Why aren't you guys wasted yet?" Max jested as he approached his skate crew with a lazy, playful smirk adorning his face.

"We're getting there!" one of the skaters called back through the noise, chugging his beer.

Max grabbed a bottle from one of the guys next to him and downed it. He tossed it like a basketball into the trash. He dabbed up the guys all around him.

"Bridger is looking for you, by the way," another skater chimed in.

"Oh! Hotshot's finally crawling back to me?" Max laughed. "Where is the fucker?"

"I think I saw him go upstairs," the skater replied.

"Uh oh! Naughty Bridge!" Max cooed with a shit-eating grin. "Did he take a girl up there?"

The guys all chortled as Max parted their crowd and eagerly jogged up the stairs to find Bridger.

The moon cast a soft glow above Gus and Bridger on the roof, giving the sense once again that they lived within their own secluded paradise under the stars. They spoke about everything and nothing all at once, their hands entwined between them.

Both boys jumped when glass shattered somewhere inside and

incited a collective cheer. They caught eyes and chuckled.

"These parties aren't really my thing," Gus admitted with a reluctant wince. "I prefer spending time with people one-on-one."

"I know. Sorry." Bridger sighed. "I'm realizing they're not as cool as I always thought. But I had to come for Max."

Gus paused. He shook his head.

"Everyone seems to owe Max something," Gus remarked.

Bridger shrugged, but then slowly nodded as he glanced up.

"If there's one thing Max is, it's loyal," Bridger explained. "If he cares about you, he's obsessed."

Gus bobbed his head back and forth, thinking.

"Are you gonna tell Max about us?" he asked.

"No way. He'd kill me," Bridger said, "*and* you." He squeezed Gus's hand and gave it a shake. "Let's just work on convincing him to let you skate with the crew first."

The boys both laughed gently, but then Gus shook his head again. "But I only have a few weeks before I leave. So, no way that's happening."

Bridger sat up, swaying with the light breeze above the neighborhood. "About that... I've been thinking. If I got a job and saved up. Could I come visit you at your school?"

"You'd do that?!"

Gus almost couldn't breathe. A glowing golden warmth flickered inside his body, like Bridger was starting to truly care about him. It was healing. It was comfort.

Is this... love?

Gus swallowed. "You don't have to."

"I want to," Bridger pressed. "I still have senior year and I've never been on a plane, but... I gotta try at least."

Gus's eyes darted between Bridger's. He softened at the sweet gesture. "Then... yes. I'd like that. Because I'll really miss you."

"Good." Bridger squared his shoulders in a put-on show of strength. "Because you can't get rid of me just by moving states, you know."

The boys shared a smile. Gus bit his lip as his gaze slowly shifted from Bridger's amber eyes to his ruby lips. Bridger's eyebrows raised as he smirked. He leaned in and kissed Gus gently. The laughter, drunken shouts, and punk rock of the party all drained away as the boys embraced, high above it all. Free of the noise, Gus felt only Bridger. Gus pushed deeper into the kiss and pulled Bridger toward him as their tentative contact began to heat up on the roof.

"Bridger! You in here?" Max pounded on a closed door down the hallway, his tone oddly more nervous than intimidating. "You screwing some chick?" he added with an unconvincing snicker. "Want me to join?"

"FUCK OFF, MAX!" a deeper voice than Bridger's growled back. It was his college friend.

Max flipped the bird at the door, then stumbled farther down the second-floor.

"I know you and some girl are hooking up around here, Bridge!" Max called out as he peered into the lit empty bedroom with the open window. He moved on. He was on a mission.

A few steps away, Max paused, processing. He took a few steps backward and looked into the lit bedroom again.

There. Bridger's new flame board—it sat side by side with that Gus kid's pansy-ass mountain board.

Max's eyebrows furrowed as he stomped into the room. He could see someone through the moving curtain and he leaned out the open window.

What. The. Fuck?!

He squinted in anger and confusion, transfixed on the two boys kissing. On Bridger. On *Gus*.

Fucking Gus.

Their limbs were so fully tangled that Max couldn't tell whose was whose. With their bodies pressed so close to swap spit, they couldn't even see him.

Max wanted to explode.

What broke him was the innocent giggle Gus let out as the boys took a moment to breathe.

Erupting with rage, Max stepped backward. Looked around. His arms were heavy with a need to act. He peered down at Bridger's board leaning against the wall. After hesitating for a moment, he snatched it and tucked it under his arm. Then he reached for Gus's board.

A lamp crashed as Max's knuckles knocked into it, sending it out of the window.

Shit!

He backed hastily out of the room and dashed down the stairs.

Gus and Bridger whipped around as something shattered behind them and the bedroom went dark. They shared a distressed look and immediately clambered back through the window to investigate.

"Shit! Someone took my board!" Bridger cursed.

"What?!"

Bridger bolted out of the bedroom, leaving Gus behind.

Party music blasted in the living room as people danced and drank. Max raced through, shoving people out of his way.

"Max!" Bridger called out from the staircase.

Max fully ignored him as he chucked Bridger's board into the living room's roaring fireplace.

"What are you doing?!" Bridger screeched. "My board! Fuck!"

Bridger raced for a fire poker and fished his skateboard out of the flames. The burning board dropped onto the hearth with a *thud*. He cursed and snatched a drink off a tipsy girl and dumped the liquid over the skateboard to put it out.

Once bright and flashy, Bridger's board was now wet, sticky, and covered in black scorch marks.

The music still played, but everyone was watching him.

Back at the foot of the staircase, Gus struggled to push past the crowd to the main room, but there were too many partygoers blocking him.

Bridger's fury rose so fast, the room spun.

Then, out of nowhere, Max slammed into Bridger so hard he crashed to his ass.

"Max!" Bridger howled.

Max picked up Bridger's scorched board and made a break

through the crowd again.

Bridger sprang to his feet to pursue his thief.

The head start got Max out the nearby screen door and into the backyard. He hurled the board far away to the ground.

"Dude, what the fuck?" Bridger bellowed as he caught up.

All around them, college students drank and danced to the music pouring from the house, the scene was so rowdy that even the arguing boys blended in.

Bridger tried to push past Max to retrieve his board, but Max wrenched him by the shirt and yanked him close. Bridger grasped Max's wrists and pulled, trying to escape his iron clutch to no avail.

"I told you!" Max screamed in Bridger's face. "You use *MY* boards, from *MY* shop. Not his!"

Bridger leaned his head back. "What the fuck are you on?!"

"Why the fuck were you sucking that fag's face?" Max's tone dropped to a crude sneer as he held Bridger tighter by the collar.

Bridger paled. *He... he saw us?*

"What?!" Bridger deflected as Max released his grasp. "What is wrong with you?"

"Me? Nothing!" Max hissed viciously. "Because I'm not fucking gay!"

Bridger's mind reeled at Max's words, his world crashing down around him. His face turned red. His eyes jumped around to see if anyone else had heard.

"Wha—? I—" He coughed. "No. I'm not!"

Undeterred, Max continued his tirade, his voice dripping with disdain. "And him?" Max thrust a finger back at the house. "*HIM?* Of all people?" Max looked at Bridger with disgust.

Only a few partygoers turned to witness the growing commotion. But Bridger began to spiral.

"And to think... we were friends." Max shook his head. "I don't even know you anymore."

"Max! You're drunk," Bridger reasoned, trying to backtrack. "You don't know what you're say—"

"I just saw it with my own eyes, you fuck," Max cut him off. "I almost vomited." He shoved Bridger in the shoulder. Bridger took it with an angry wince.

"I let you skate with me for years. *Years!* And you were lying to me the entire time," Max accused, towering over Bridger. "All you were doing was looking at us guys, checking us out. You disgusting fuck!"

"No. Not at all. I—"

"Take your fag boyfriend and get the fuck out of my party!" Max knocked Bridger to the ground again. Bridger groaned as he hit the muddy grass. Max twisted away.

"Pathetic," Max muttered under his breath. "You always were useless."

Bridger glared up at his former friend. He stood up quickly, grabbed Max's retreating arm to drag him close, and punched him square in the face.

Max recoiled in shock. His nose immediately poured blood.

"Fuck you, you little twerp," Max snarled.

Max punched Bridger back, aiming for his jaw. Bridger caught the fist, and the two scrabbled and fell to the grass. Max, exerting all his strength, pinned Bridger down with his knees. He wailed on Bridger over and over, pounding on him with unforgiving blows.

Max grunted in anger as onlookers whispered in fear. They did nothing, even as Bridger's whimpers went quiet. Bridger's gaze was fading, his head hurt. He couldn't fight back anymore.

Bang! A skateboard crashed into Max's skull, *hard*.

Max crumpled to the muddy ground. Gus stood behind him, his homemade board clutched in his hands.

Lying in the dirt, motionless, Max dripped blood from a gash on the back of his head.

The few drunk people nearby—seeing how very south this fight had gone—scattered. No one helped any of the boys.

Gus dropped to Bridger's side. "Bridger? Bridger, are you okay?" His voice cracked.

Bridger coughed. His gums were growing bloody. He clutched his ribs and groaned.

Slowly, Gus helped Bridger to his feet. The boy was heavy and dragging. Gus tucked both their boards under his right arm and weaved his other around Bridger's middle to clumsily hold him up.

Chaos swirled all around them. Gus had no idea what he was going to do, only that he had to get Bridger out of here. Together, both boys limped away from the backyard toward the front of the house.

Bursting from the front door, Tara spotted Gus as he shouldered Bridger toward the street.

"Gus!" Tara called out to him. "What happened?"

Gus didn't hear Tara as he pushed past the beer-filled kids on the front lawn.

Tara, frowning, twisted to look toward the far-off backyard. There, she saw Max's splayed drunk frame on the ground. She shook her head in anger and disappointment.

This was nothing new.

Chapter 14

Goodbye

Terrified, Gus guided the wounded Bridger to a roadside bench a block away. Bridger sucked air through his clenched teeth as he was carefully set down on the weather-worn seat. He groaned and dropped his head into his hands, overwhelmed. Gus set their boards beside the curb.

Tears welled in Bridger's eyes. He struggled to fight them back. "Why did you do that?!"

"Why did I—what do you mean *why*?" Gus watched the back of Bridger's drooping head, unable to look away from the bloody mess of him. "I saved you."

"This saved *nothing*!" Bridger yelled, looking up with wet eyes. His already swollen jaw wobbled. "Max saw us!"

"Saw us?" Gus questioned.

"On the roof, Gus. On the roof!" Bridger hissed back.

Gus cursed under his breath.

Bridger wiped his bloody nose as he growled in anguish and

frustration. His every exhale was heavy with fear, regret, and pain.

Gus reached for him.

Bridger recoiled. "Get away from me!"

Gus bit the inside of his cheek, then shook his head. "No, Bridger. We need to leave," Gus insisted. "Now."

"Where the fuck am I going to go, Gus?!" Bridger snapped. "Max is gonna tell everyone!"

Gus sat down next to his friend. Bridger scooted away, his built-up tears streaming free.

"Fuck. My *parents* are gonna find out!" Bridger slammed his own thigh.

"It's okay," Gus tried to calm him down. "We'll figure something—"

"This was all a fuckin' mistake!" Bridger burst out, cutting him off.

Gus's train of thought sped away as his stomach sank.

The boys sat in silence. The booming party music from down the street reverberated as if the house were a trashy club.

"Everything?" Gus slowly asked. "*Everything* was a mistake?"

Bridger kept his chin down. Gus leaned in, moving his face to try and catch Bridger's eyes for any possible reassurance, but Bridger avoided his gaze.

"Do you mean *me*, too?"

"Yeah, Gus. All of it," Bridger said to the ground. "I'm sorry."

"C'mon," Gus pressed, trying to keep his voice light despite his constricting throat and heaving chest. "You don't mean that."

Bridger couldn't bear to even shift in Gus's direction. Irritated, he shook a head full of doubts.

"I'm not like you," Bridger said softly, still staring at the dirty street. "All This? Here? This is my *life*, Gus."

Finally, Bridger lifted his chin, regarding Gus with puffy eyes. His nose dripped blood and snot.

"This is all easier for you," Bridger said. "You only just got here, and you're leaving soon. But me? I'll always be stuck with these people. In this town." Bridger waved an arm in front of him. "And now everything is ruined. I can never skate with the guys again."

"But... skating isn't everything," Gus tried his best to comfort.

Bridger's mouth fell open. Gus's jumbled encouragement had him confused. Disgusted, even. He couldn't shake the thought that maybe this boy didn't even know him at all.

"What?! I'll have no one, Gus! Or don't you realize that?" Bridger wailed. "Without Max, without *skating*... who even am I?"

"I didn't mean—I'm sorry. Keep skating." Gus thrust a hand back toward the party. "But *that's* not all you have. Just ignore Max. Who cares what he thinks?"

"Everybody!" Bridger replied, his voice strained. "Everybody cares what he thinks!."

"Not forever," Gus said, trying to level his tone. "That won't last. He's twenty-three but still hangs out with teenagers. If you leave Livingston, he's nothing to you. There's so much more you can do away from here."

Bridger shook his head, fully drained. Gus wasn't getting it. Maybe he never would.

"Gus." Bridger tried to push severity into his words as he locked pained eyes with him. "I'm. Not. Like. You. I don't think I'll ever get out of this town."

The air felt cold and damp. Gus's own tears slipped down his clammy cheeks.

Is that what he really means? Why he wants us to be over? Because we're too different?

"You might..." Gus offered hopelessly. "One day."

Still, Bridger's shoulders fell even more. He sighed and shook his head. He said nothing else.

"Even if you never leave," Gus pushed on, "what I really meant was... skating isn't *all* you've got. You're great at other stuff, too."

"Psh. Like what?"

Gus scoffed back with a tearful smirk. "You're kidding."

"What?" Bridger broke from his depressed tone.

"Okay. For starters, do you even remember the bonfire? How much people love your stories? Bridger, they can listen to you talk, just *talk*, for hours."

"So? That doesn't matter," Bridger dismissed.

"Yes, it does!"

Bridger squinted, tilted his face, and turned back up to Gus.

"Also, convincing my dad to sell the boards? That was *your* idea. The flyers? *Your* idea. I never would've thought of those things," Gus pointed out. "You're charming. Confident. You make things *happen*!"

Bridger wiped some tears away. Gus leaned in.

"You once told me that you don't want to think about the future," Gus said slowly. "That you only want to focus on this summer, on *right now*."

"Was I drunk?" Bridger half-joked, and rubbed his aching ribs.

Gus didn't laugh. He stared deep into Bridger's gaze.

"All the small moments you love so much won't last very long," Gus admitted gently, thinking about his mother. "But that means neither will these bad ones. Eventually, no one's gonna even remember tonight. Things have to get better."

"I don't... want things to end," Bridger confessed. He'd straightened up some. Loosened.

"I know. But... we can't stop it. *Right now* can't last forever. You showed me life goes by *so* fast. And that's a good thing. A great thing!" Gus reassured him. "The rush... it's worth some falls."

Bridger shook his head with a chuckle. "I'm not ready for all this grown-up shit," he jested.

Gus laughed. "Same." He reached warmly for Bridger's shoulder. "But at least we're not alone... right?"

Bridger hesitated. He looked at Gus's face, at how serious he seemed about this. At how much he seemed to care. Recognizing that someone *knew* him... it felt good. He didn't want to lose it.

Bridger accepted Gus's gentle touch.

"You are not a mistake." Bridger straightened up. His eyes were still watery, but the resolve in them was growing firm. "I take it back. The truth is... I need you. Especially now. My life's about to be shit."

Gus melted. "I need you, too." He rubbed Bridger's back. "The *real* you, as you are. That's enough."

Bridger nodded with a painful grimace.

"Thanks, Gus," he said softly.

"We'll get through this." Gus promised him.

Nodding, Bridger wrapped Gus in a deep hug. And Gus inhaled the comforting relief of being back in Bridger's embrace where he belonged.

The boys squeezed each other tight on the wooden bench under the warm yellow street light. They both turned to face each other and softly, slowly, kissed the unease away.

When they parted, all was okay.

Before Gus could even wonder what they should do next, Bridger shot up from his seat.

"Follow me."

"Why?" Gus chuckled when Bridger just smirked in response. "What are you up to?"

Bridger bent down to snag his skateboard and hopped on. He gave it a few test flips, nodded, then winked at Gus before speeding off down the dimly lit suburban road.

"Let's go skate!" Bridger called back over his shoulder.

Gus shot up with excitement, grabbed his board, and followed behind his skater boy.

Max rolled awake in the party house's backyard, disoriented and covered in torn-up grass and dirt. He put his hand to the back of his head in pain, confused by the blood that came away on his fingers.

"Ugh," he groaned quietly, clutching his head.

Max inched to his feet. He spotted a half-empty red cup nearby and downed a messy swig.

Behind Max, Tara Shae stormed out from the back of the party house, tossed an unfinished beer in the trash, and rushed toward her car.

"Tara! Where ya going?" Max called out to her, "The party's not over."

Tara ignored him.

"You didn't even say goodbye yet." Max stumbled after her, tipsy, bloody, and sweaty.

Tara took a breath and turned around in the street to face Max.

"You were an asshole to everyone tonight," Tara fumed, clearly annoyed. "Especially Gus and Bridger. I'm going home."

"Who cares about those fucks?! It's my birthday. Don't leave yet," Max insisted.

"What? Am I supposed to bake you a cake?" Tara shot back.

Max shrugged with a hiccup and a smugly flirtatious smile. "That'd be cute. Why not?"

"Because that's not me at all, Max," Tara stated seriously. "I've never been like that."

Max rolled his eyes. Tara looked like she wanted to say more but stopped herself.

"C'mon, Tara. I know you. And you know me. So stay," Max pleaded.

"No, you don't *know me*," Tara expressed, pain in her eyes. "You don't, and you stopped caring a long time ago."

Max looked perplexed. "Yeah, well I—"

"And I don't understand *you* anymore either," Tara added, gesturing to all of Max's drunkard self in the street. "*This* isn't the Max I used to know."

"Tara..."

"You need to grow up." She stood her ground. "We're not kids anymore. Stop drinking and stop being so angry all the time. *You* are the one making everything harder on yourself."

"Take me back, then." Max softened. "Babe, everything can go back to the way it was. I *miss* you."

"No. I don't want to go *back*," Tara replied incredulously. "I can't do that."

"Why? I can be better, I promise," Max insisted.

"You've said that before."

"I mean it this time. I—"

"Max, it can't happen. And I don't want..." Tara struggled to find the right words. "To say this here... like this..."

A sad silence drifted down between the two ex-lovers. Two distant, broken friends.

"Tara, I still love you. You're the only real friend I've ever had," Max confessed.

She looked up at him, saddened pity and regret in her eyes, and debated if she should reveal what she wanted to or just leave. In the end, she shook her head sadly. "I have to tell you something—"

Max lunged forward and kissed Tara forcefully.

Tara's face exploded in shock as his lips clutched hers, and she quickly shoved him off. He almost fell over.

"Ugh! Friends don't do *that*!" Tara exclaimed, exasperated.

Though he'd regained his footing, Max stumbled as he shook his head at her. "I thought—"

"Max, I'm moving to California and... I'm..." Tara struggled over how to put her secret into delicate words. She breathed in, swallowed deeply, and locked her knees to look up at her old boyfriend. "I can't be with you like you want. Not now, not ever."

"What?" Max was stunned, as if he'd been clubbed again by a second skateboard.

There was dead silence. Tara and Max stared lost in each other's eyes with opposite forms of heartbreak. Max looked like a wounded puppy, and Tara had to shake away the tear that dripped down her cheek.

"There's more." Tara bolstered herself. "I should've told you this back when—"

"Has everyone gone insane?!" Max yelled again.

Tara barely flinched. She swallowed her reveal in the wake of Max's aggression and laughed in disbelief. She wiped another stupid tear away and shook her head as Max raged on. He didn't deserve to know. Not like this.

"Everything was perfect a few years ago. It's all shit now!" Max screamed, throwing his arm back to point at the party house. "Nobody back there actually cares about me. The store is failing. And now you're leaving Montana? I can't—"

"Shut up, Max! Just shut *up*!" Tara interrupted fiercely. "Your life doesn't suck because everything is different now. It's because you refuse to move on!"

Max froze. He narrowed his eyes, hurt and bewildered.

Tara stepped back and took an exhausted breath. "We used to spend every day together. And I—I really enjoyed my time with you. I did. And I *did* used to love you. But I started realizing that...

I could never love you the way you loved me."

Max, for once, waited to speak.

Tara took another deep breath. "I need to start living my own life, the way I want, for *me*," she said firmly.

She stepped forward and peeled off her old favorite snapback she was gifted long ago. She'd worn this one special, just for tonight. Max quickly moved his gaze down and away from her as his sobs broke through. His ruined birthday party blared behind him.

Tara reached out, returning her vibrant ruby-red snapback to its original owner, Max.

"No. I don't want it back," he muttered, entirely crushed.

Tara sighed and lowered his hat down by her side. The pained stillness between them buzzed like the cicadas.

"I leave in September," Tara said. "I need time, but if you figure your shit out, if you *heal*, come visit me. I'll share more of... who I am now. We can skate together. *As friends.*"

Hunched over and gritting his teeth, Max couldn't speak. He just studied the ground.

Tara nodded to herself, reached up, and put the snapback on Max's head. She wiped away a spot of blood from his temple.

Max kept his chin down, unable to hold back a fresh flood of tears.

"Goodbye, Max," Tara said softly.

She stepped back and headed to her car. Once inside, she closed the door, blocking Max out.

Tara drove away. Max stood alone, crying in the road.

A deep sapphire sky of glowing constellations sparkled above Gus and Bridger as they skated down the barren night streets outside Livingston. A breeze rushed through empty trees as birds settled down to slumber in their shared nests. Bridger stretched out his arms, soaring through the evening wind. Gus followed suit, falling in love with the fast-paced sensation Bridger enjoyed so much.

"Fresh air never felt so good!" Bridger exclaimed.

The boys continued to weave back and forth between each other under the moonlight. They relished this short, quick ride to end their too-long day. Because they had stuck together, this dangerous night had somehow become beautiful.

It was so late it was almost morning when Bridger drove Gus home. As they approached Dan's cabin, Bridger clocked the empty driveway. His stomach soared with new excitement.

"Is your dad not home?" Bridger asked. "Will he be out long?"

Gus blushed. "He's on a fishing trip in Yellowstone until tomorrow."

Bridger pulled into the empty graveled parking space and turned off the engine.

"Good. I've been craving some alone time with you." Bridger gave Gus a cheeky look.

Gus blushed even harder.

The boys burst through the cabin door, already heatedly making out. They stumbled through the house, bumping into furniture. They kicked off their shoes while their hands stayed busy in each other's hair or on each other's body.

They parted only to rush up the stairs to Gus's bedroom. As soon as they entered, Bridger gently pushed Gus up against the wooden wall. They kissed deeper and slower. Hot passion filled every corner of the small attic room. Finally, both needing a moment to breathe, Bridger and Gus paused kissing. They opened their eyes, looking deeply at each other.

"Sure you want to do this?" Bridger asked through raspy breaths. "It's—it's my first time."

Gus bit his lip, smiling. "Yeah. Mine too. But yeah. I'm sure."

Bridger smiled back. "Are you nervous?" He flushed. "...I am."

"I'm... somehow not." Gus laughed in disbelief, his eyes sparkling. "Not with you."

Gus stepped closer and lifted Bridger's shirt with steady hands. Bridger raised his eyebrows, surprised and aroused by Gus's newfound confidence.

Gus dropped Bridger's shirt to the floor and unbuttoned his polo. The boys shared a heated look as the garment came off each of Gus's shoulders.

Bridger slowly scanned Gus's naked torso. His skin looked so soft, so inviting. The months of woodworking and skateboarding had earned Gus a visible definition to muscles that Bridger now hungered to touch and taste.

Gus blushed at Bridger's aroused eyes. He followed Bridger's hands as the skater boy took a step back and undid the button of his pants and unzipped his jeans. Gus's heart skipped a beat. The strong shirtless body before him rippled in a mesmerizing contortion as Bridger bent to push his pants down and off.

As Bridger stood back up, Gus saw on him the same underwear Bridger flashed outside TJ's during their first days together. Gus had pictured these same boxers more times than he could count. Now Gus desperately desired to finally see more than just Bridger's hidden beer bottle. The young man standing in front of Gus was everything he'd yearned for in secret all summer long. His lean and chiseled body, his alluring scent, his lustful gaze—all were finally tangible before him, no longer just in Gus's sketchy imagination.

The craving between them was almost too much for the boys to handle.

"Woah..." Gus let out.

"Yeah," Bridger breathed.

Bridger stepped languidly forward, closing the distance between them. He took Gus's wrists in his hands and placed them on his hips, dragging Gus closer again.

"Wait," Gus said in a laugh against Bridger's lips.

Gus reached down and undid his belt, getting rid of his own pants. A jolt of energy surged through him as Bridger reached behind him and firmly squeezed his butt.

Crackling with need, Gus pulled Bridger toward his bed. As they lowered onto the mattress, both boys met kiss for kiss. Gus wrapped his arms around Bridger's back and drew him in as tight as he could atop his soft blankets.

A glorious few minutes of making out passed, and Gus felt Bridger's hand slide down along his chest and stomach to grasp his stiffening member over his briefs. Gus gasped in pleasure, and Bridger chuckled with lustful joy into their kiss. He squeezed Gus's dick and began to stroke it over the material. Gus released a low moan of delight, and Bridger caught his lip between his teeth. They parted briefly, and Gus relished Bridger's gleeful expression. Their eye contact was electric.

"Can't believe I'm about to do this," Gus's skater boy said.

Gus stretched forward and kissed Bridger, hard.

Bridger slipped his tongue into Gus's mouth, savoring the taste of him. Then his kisses moved to Gus's chin, to his neck, the hollow of his throat, slowly trailing down his body. He lingered on Gus's nipples, slid his tongue down his stomach, pressed his open mouth lithely against his pelvis.

Every muscle in Gus's body quivered.

When Bridger reached below Gus's waist, he pulled at the band of his blue briefs. With a nervous smirk and a raised eyebrow, Bridger looked up at Gus, who nodded.

"Yes. Please, yes," Gus said.

Bridger ripped the briefs down Gus's legs. He reached back between Gus's bare thighs and squeezed his exposed penis again.

"You are... really fucking sexy," Bridger laughed.

Then Bridger slid down and took all of Gus into his mouth.

Gus gasped.

Oh! Oh...

The boy couldn't think. Couldn't breathe. Couldn't *live* because *this* was better. This was all the ecstasy of loving and being loved, all the pleasure of needing and being needed.

Gus struggled to focus as Bridger kept going but hummed in joy when he glanced down to see Bridger thoroughly enjoying himself.

He couldn't wait to inspect every single inch of Bridger with his own mouth in time.

It was a night of firsts—flashes of skin, the laughter from mess-ups, the intoxicating slick of sweat sheening their tangled bodies.

The attic bedroom brimmed with their deep intimacy, their unbridled pleasure. All night long, until morning dawned, the boys played and explored each other's beautiful bodies.

Angry, depressed, and now even more drunk, Max entered his small family home after leaving his birthday party and slammed the door behind him. His mother's boyfriend, Jay, who was sitting on the couch, spilled his beer on himself in shock.

The drunk men started to scream at each other, just like most other nights. Max's mom walked into the room, covering her ears as she attempted to stop them. She was pushed away—by which of them, it wasn't quite clear—and started crying.

Around them, bills were piled up on a counter. Stacks of skateboard products sat unsold in boxes along the walls.

"—a faggot, that's all you are," Jay finally screamed. He slugged Max across the chin.

Max clutched his bruising face and stormed off, slamming his bedroom door.

The boy sat on his bed and clenched his fists, seething with anger. Jay resigned himself to screaming at his mother instead.

Max lay back on his mattress and stared blankly at his ceiling. Taped-up posters of pro skateboarders and far-off cities there taunted him, their promised escape plan an impossible fantasy. Clutching his pillow, Max turned to the end table on his left. There, on the nightstand, sat an old framed photo of him as a child with his mother and deceased father.

Max had never noticed this portrait in the house while his dad was still alive. But the day after his father was gone, it stood out, another frozen memory of the man he refused to let anyone take from him. Max had come to cherish this photo like a holy relic, always keeping it near. It was the forgotten past peace of his *true* family that welcomed him to sleep each night.

Taped to the portrait were two unframed pictures: one of Bridger, one of Tara. The only two people Max had thought actually cared about him anymore. Young, pretty Tara wore his red snapback in her high school graduation photo and Bridger was flipping off Max's camera with his signature smirk of wild rebellion. These two images never failed to make Max smile before. Now both brought him pain. Tears streamed down Max's cheeks. He was forever trapped in this life without them.

Why does everyone leave me?

This town, this home, this life. It was all his prison.

"FUCK!"

All his pent-up rage carried him from his mattress, and he chucked his skateboard across his bedroom. It bounced off his dark walls and crashed into the outdated Dell on his desk. The screen cracked. The machine fell to the ground, dead.

Max screamed at the top of his lungs.

He screamed until nothing else could come out.

Heaving with exerted energy and burning with self-loathing, Max smacked his own forehead again and again as tears leaked down.

Fuck this. Fuck me. I'm so fucked up. I'm fucking broken. What is wrong with me?

Jay pounded on his bedroom door.

"What the fuck is going on in there?"

Luckily, Max had locked him out. He had locked everyone out.

As both poundings continued. Max's tear-stained face morphed from anger to apathy.

He stared blankly across his room. Everything became nothing.

And nothing hurt most when you were alone.

Max lowered himself back into his bed. He pulled up his covers, closed his eyes, and wept as his mom's boyfriend continued to bang on the door and shout even louder.

But he heard nothing anymore. Nothing at all.

Chapter 15

The Same Mistakes

The next morning, Gus woke with his arm dangling off the side of his bed. He yawned, stretching wide to rouse all the sore muscles he used last night.

Last night.

Gus's eyes flashed open. He gasped, thinking.

Was it all real? Or did I just dream it?

Gus didn't want to look. He didn't want to know the colorful magic of last night may have just been another picture he'd drawn in his mind.

A loud snore sounded behind him.

Gus flipped to his other side. There, lying next to him in bed, shirtless and cloaked in the golden light of sunrise, was his hand-some Bridger.

The skater boy snored again.

Gus smiled contentedly, scooted farther down beneath the covers, and laid his head on Bridger's warm chest. He inhaled

Bridger's tangy night sweat and crisp deodorant, and exhaled a deep, calming breath, finally at home in this Montana cabin.

He draped his arm over Bridger's torso and lifted his leg over his lover's thigh. Beneath him, Gus felt Bridger slowly stir awake.

"Good morning," Gus greeted with a smile of relief.

Bridger smirked with sparkling eyes as he found Gus. "Morning." He yawned happily.

Grinning, Gus kissed Bridger's forehead as two happy birds chirped outside.

"Your bed's so cozy..." Bridger spoke gently. "I'm glad I stuck around."

Gus and Bridger eventually got dressed and walked downstairs to the kitchen. As Gus went to grab some food, the phone rang. Dan rushed in from outside with a clipboard in hand and a pencil tucked above his ear, befuddled but delighted to see the boys in the kitchen.

"People have been calling all morning mentioning *flyers*? Saying they're excited to buy boards?" Dan studied their pleased expressions. "What did you two do?"

Last night flashed in Gus's head. *Lots.*

He and Bridger shared a charged look, then chuckled.

Oh, he means the flyers...

"Somebody's good for business," Gus finally said, pointing to a smiling Bridger as the phone rang again.

"Okay. Well, you gonna get that?" Dan inquired.

Still laughing, Gus scrambled to answer.

Gus talked with the new customer on the phone while Bridger handed him a notepad so he could take down their first public orders. The entire rest of the day, the three men collaborated on a new round of skateboards. At dusk, Bridger put down his tools, hugged Gus goodbye, and headed home.

Dan watched them part. He crossed his arms in thought.

Something was different between the boys.

Later that evening, Dan and Gus sat down for a meal of grilled venison, roasted red potatoes, and cheddar creamed corn.

Mid-dinner, Dan raised his beer to Gus.

"You did good today, kid," Dan praised. "You earned the weekend off."

"I thought we were finishing more boards?" Gus asked.

"They can wait until Monday," Dan said.

Gus nodded his delight. "Okay! Sweet!" Already, he began wondering how he'd spend the extra days of freedom.

As Gus downed a few more mouthfuls of venison, Dan continued to watch his son.

"So, from today, I gather everything's patched up with Bridger?" Dan asked.

Gus snorted. "Yeah. Definitely."

"Glad you were able to make a good friend before the summer ended," Dan commented.

At the word *friend*, Gus paused. He nodded slowly, poking a potato.

Tell him, something inside him urged.

Gus watched his father as the man drank his beer.

"Uh... Dad?" Gus started tentatively. His leg bounced under the table.

"Humpfrh," Dan acknowledged while still eating.

"I... have to tell you something," Gus said, taking a deep breath.

"I'm all ears."

"I—I think I wanna be with Bridger."

"You should," Dan agreed, wiping his mouth with a napkin. "Bridger is a good kid. Hard worker."

Gus shook his head. "I... don't think you're getting it."

"No, I fully understand," Dan said.

"We're... more than friends now," Gus confessed.

Dan went silent for a moment. He regarded his son quietly.

"Well, say something," Gus urged, a hint of desperation in his voice.

A long, still pause hit the table. Dan was unflinching, almost as if paralyzed with indecision.

Gus had never seen him like this.

"Dad? Please don't be upset," Gus pleaded softly.

Dan took a deep breath and put his silverware down.

"Gus... life can be... lonely," he began, his voice slow, choosing each word intentionally.

He cleared his throat and looked off, lost in contemplation. Then his glance came back to a nervous Gus.

"When I met your mom, I was still at the mill. She always came in asking us for scrap wood to make canvases, but my boss said no. Even after she offered a landscape painting in exchange." Dan slowly grew a grin full of happy memories. "This *gorgeous* view of an elk drinking from a brook. It reminded me of home, of peace. So I snuck her a wood bundle for the painting. She was back the next week with another, and it... became our thing.

"Months later, I got the courage to ask her over for dinner." Dan smiled at his son. "She loved my pot roast and garlic potatoes, just like you do.

"We got married. But working at the mill... my body was breaking from those twelve-hour days. Your mom inspired me to open my own shop." Dan laughed. "It was a rough start. I worked twice as much. I didn't sleep. I'd drink. We would fight," he revealed, adjusting in his chair uncomfortably. "And then you came along. I had no other way of providing for both of you. I knew Mom would stay with me, keep us together, even when times got tough."

Dan tapped the table as so many regrets flooded back to his brain.

"But then one day... she left. Your mom left, and she took you with her." Dan's gaze shifted to his empty walls. "And I couldn't stop her. I lost her, I lost you. I was alone. And I realized then, that I have zero control over... anything."

Gus had stopped eating, the weight of this conversation too heavy to move beneath. His stoic lumberjack dad never wanted to talk about his mom. Yet here he was, sharing all of these things Gus had never known. All because of him and Bridger?

"Then she got sick, and I didn't have time to fly out and help her... I can never take those mistakes back."

Dan looked at Gus, trying to stay strong.

"She was my person," Dan concluded, his eyes damp.

Gus averted his eyes as if it could stop his own tears from falling as he thought about his mom.

"I'm not blind. You and Bridger. Don't let me stop you. Enjoy it, *now*, while you have it. Or you'll always regret the days and years you missed out on... and wish you could do it all over again," Dan advised, his voice dripping with lost time.

Gus took a deep, shuddering breath. His dad *did* understand. He understood about Bridger, and it meant more than Gus could ever have thought it would.

"It's *hard* to find someone." Dan's shoulders sank in sadness. "So... you're damn lucky,"

Gus looked at his father, finally comprehending why the aging man had stayed so lonely.

Dan nodded with the weight of so many lost chances as he looked at his own reflection in his son. "Even love can end."

Gus leaned forward and put his hand on his dad's arm. Dan closed his eyes and finally let his buried tears fall.

"Mom needed to be on her own, but I know... she never stopped loving you," Gus said softly.

Dan looked up at his son as a reluctant tear slowly dropped. He stood up and pulled Gus in for a deep hug. Their first real hug in years.

Gus squeezed his dad tight beside the dining room table.

They held the hug for a rare, long time.

"I'm proud of you," Dan said finally.

Teary Gus grinned in his father's embrace.

Dan turned to look again at the empty nails on the walls.

That night, Gus drove out to the skatepark to meet up with Bridger. They sat under the same streetlight they met under, chatting, skating, laughing, and kissing. Telling his father even just the smallest inkling of his relationship with Bridger had given Gus a sense of freedom and peace he hadn't known he'd needed.

With Gus out with Bridger well into the evening, Dan had the cabin all to himself. He was used to this, but tonight it felt more mirthless than ever. So many good memories, tainted by his old mistakes. Instead of watching television before bed like every other night, Dan walked upstairs.

Dan opened the door to Gus's bedroom. He gazed at the mattress no longer covered in the adorable childhood blanket of horses and cowboys. He remembered the late nights, checking in, when his young son slept there as a little boy. Dan walked through the space toward his locked wooden trunk he had hid here thirteen years ago. He sighed deeply and lowered to his knees before it. His eyes went distant with thought.

Dan took the keys from his back pocket and undid the trunk's padlock. With his hands shaking, he lifted the lid to reveal what was inside. The box was stuffed to the brim with his late wife's unfinished paintings, sketches, drawings, and art materials she had left behind. The sight of each item brought back vivid scenes and Megan's favorite inspirations—brought back the stories she'd tell him through her creations. A fresh gash of pain sliced open as Dan remembered Gus's torn sketchbook.

Dan moved some papers in the chest to find the elk painting that brought him and Megan together, and lifted it up to admire it. It caught the light in just the right way that the image looked *real*. Like he was seeing a distant elk with giant antlers peacefully watching him through the painted forest.

Still just as beautiful.

He set the canvas down. He picked out some wood-bound books he had put together for his wife over a decade ago and set them on the nearby end table.

Stacked between other keepsakes stored in the trunk, Dan spotted a photograph. He stared into the forgotten image of him with his arm wrapped around Megan's shoulders. Beneath it were many other photos of the couple and some of them with baby Gus, each moment happy and full of love.

He stared back into the preserved past: him, his wife, his son.

So much time I lost.

Dan laid the framed photo down slowly. His head fell back as the tears streamed down.

Gus and Bridger tried to keep their public life as normal as possible even though they'd essentially betrayed the king of Livingston. However, it would have been impossible for Gus clubbing Max Stevens in the head with his skateboard to not bring about some unfortunate repercussions.

Skating at McNair, for one, was awkwardly tense. Max, when he finally did show a few days after his birthday, flaunted an unbandaged, scabbed temple. Gus had wanted to apologize, but Bridger insisted they had no need.

"He made his choice," Bridger had told Gus when they took a break from skating under a tree. "Max started everything. He gave me way more bruises than you did him."

Bridger glared at Max from across the park. The boy didn't look back at him. Gus could feel their palpable tension even from opposite ends of the concrete.

"Plus, I know Avery and them are cool, but it's only a matter of time until Max tells the rest of the crew that you and I are... dating," Bridger said.

Gus's gaze jumped from Max's crew to Bridger.

"We're *dating*?" Gus poked Bridger, who sported a rare blush and rolled his eyes.

"I mean, yeah." Bridger said. "We better be."

Gus smiled. "Good."

After a moment, Gus had tapped Bridger's leg. "Are you gonna be okay if he does tell other people?" Gus whispered.

Bridger paused to think about it. It didn't take him too long.

"Well, I don't want people to treat me different," Bridger shrugged. "But no, I'm not afraid of people knowing you're my boyfriend, Gus."

The boys shared wide smiles. Gus had wanted to kiss Bridger so badly, but the park still didn't feel a safe space to do so, not with all the eyes on them.

Because of the fight, the crew had split in half. Allegiances seemed in flux, but Coop, Avery, and Bennet decided to stay loyal to Bridger. One point in Bridger's favor that Max's side didn't have was Tara and her friends, who liked Gus.

Today, Tara was skating with Gus while some of her friends sat on the bowl to watch.

"Tara, let's go eat," Sophia called out, bored. "I'm starving."

Tara landed her backside 180 ollie, then looked up to Sophia and Kelly.

"Mark's?" she asked. Sophia nodded. Tara then looked at Gus. "Wanna come?"

"Yeah," Gus answered. "Bridger?"

"No, you guys go." Bridger waved happily. "I'm still trying to add to this kickflip."

Gus nodded and grabbed his board. Tara's friends stood up from the concrete.

"Can I come?" Bennet popped right behind Sophia.

"Shit!" She jumped with surprise. "What do you think, *noob*?" She put her hand on her hip.

Bennet backed away, knowing the answer.

"That's right." Sophia stood firm. "Gus only."

As Sophia grabbed Tara's arm, linking theirs to walk. Kelly looked back at Bennet and blushed.

Bennet caught the girl's eye and brightened. Kelly turned away again. Bennet visibly celebrated once she had walked off.

"Bye, see you later," Gus said to Bridger, smiling.

"Yeah." Bridger smiled back. His eyes fluttered with an idea. He anxiously glanced around the park as if double-checking something.

Gus looked around. "What?"

"Come here," Bridger said briskly.

He pulled Gus in and gave him a quick peck on the lips under the tree right in front of Coop, Bennet, and Avery. Even though the three boys knew Gus and Bridger had hooked up, their mouths still fell open.

Gus giggled in surprise, flattered Bridger wasn't afraid to show him affection around his friends.

Bridger pushed him away with a wink. "Have fun. I'll meet you there as soon as I get this trick." He knocked on his flame board, refinished now after Max's freakout. It would always have its scorch marks, burned in from the day of his beating, but Bridger told Gus he liked it better that way. It was more dangerous. Badass.

Gus nodded at Bridger, then walked off with Tara and her friends.

Bridger scanned the park again to make sure none of the other locals had seen him kiss Gus and then continued to skate with Coop, Bennet, and Avery. The three friends joshed him up with playful punches about him and Gus.

However, far in the distance, at the other end of the park, one person had caught the entire romantic exchange with his stealthy eagle eye. Max Stevens had glared at Bridger and Gus's kiss with intense jealousy. He shook his head as he looked down at the board under his feet. *Kissing? HERE? In front of everybody?* Max glanced up and watched Gus walk off with Tara. He scoffed. *That twerp gets to be with Tara* and *Bridger. Utter. Horseshit.*

Max seethed as his sycophantic skate crew sped past him over and over, blocking his view of his targets. Max moved his head to eyeball Gus as he walked away from Bridger with Tara leading the way. Standing there with his sore head and jaw, Max felt the deeper pain of both Bridger's betrayal and Tara's goodbye all over again.

How the fuck am I losing them like this?

Tara's words came rushing back into Max's mind.

It's because you refuse to move on.

The days passed. Most of them, Bridger spent with Gus, woodworking and skateboarding. Today, though, Bridger arrived at McNair Skatepark early to practice alone. He often waited for Gus or his other friends to arrive as a group, but he needed some time free from distractions to work on still trying to land his new trick. He had been aiming for a varial kickflip body varial this entire summer, and focusing on Gus had pushed the goal to the wayside. But not today. He wanted to nail this trick and show it to Gus this afternoon after his work shift.

Bridger stepped onto the concrete with his board of flames in hand. He pulled his MP3 player out of his pocket, put his earbuds in, and started bobbing his head to "Best Kept Secret" by Skillet. Bridger pushed off on his board, hyperfocused as he gained speed along with the music. He skated down the concrete bumps of the pump track and circled the entire park. As he swung back around to the flat area, Bridger set up the risky jump. He popped the tail, scooped the back, and flicked his front foot to rotate the board beneath him in the air.

But as his body spun around, the board dipped dangerously sideways, and Bridger bailed. He ran off his momentum as his board rolled away. He followed it and picked it up to try the maneuver again.

Bridger circled the park, jumped, and failed. He tried again. Failed. Tried. Failed. He kept attempting but bailed each time. Bridger just couldn't stick the landing on the rare move. His boys would be arriving soon. Today might not be his day.

As Bridger rounded the south bend to build up speed for one final attempt, he placed his feet on the tail of the board, inhaled in preparation, and leaped into the air. He successfully flipped the board beneath him and shifted his position to land correctly. He stuck the landing! Then the board shot out from under his feet.

Bridger hit the concrete hard.

"Fuck!" Bridger cursed under his breath. *So close!*

Lying on his back, he groaned.

Bridger heard his *SCRAPS* board stop rolling and footsteps approaching. Still on the ground, he lifted his head.

It was Max, shuffling his way, the board under his arm.

Shit...

They still hadn't spoken since the incident. Max still had a bruise from where Gus had walloped him at his birthday party.

The menacing skater clutched Bridger's board like a weapon.

Fuck! Bridger flinched and crawled backward in fear.

The other boy stopped right above Bridger, towering over him. "Get up," Max demanded.

Bridger stayed on the ground, petrified. He considered yelling for help but, shooting his eyes this way and that, saw no one. *Fuck! Where is everyone today?* He looked back up at Max. He couldn't tell if the skater would chuck the board across the park or hit him with it.

Instead, Max extended his arm and offered the board like an olive branch.

"I told you to get up, choad. And do it one more time." Max shook his head. "You got this."

Bridger blinked. Max gave the board a shake, trying to hand it over peacefully.

Is this a trick? What the fuck is he on about?

Max offered the faintest smirk and extended the board once more.

Bridger's eyes flickered again with uncertainty, but he pushed himself up off his hands to stand up. He squinted at Max as he gently grabbed the board made by Gus, Max's enemy this summer. Max and Bridger both held the skateboard together for a moment, their eyes locked in a wordless exchange.

Max's shoulders dropped and he puffed out air thick with regret. His eyes said "Sorry" without him uttering a single word. He simply nodded sorrowfully at Bridger. Looking down at the board he tried to destroy, Max let go.

Bridger accepted the board into his own hands. He dropped it to the ground and slowly mounted it with one foot. Max took a step forward and leaned in close to Bridger's ear.

"We're the same, me and you," Max whispered.

Bridger refused to look at Max. He forced his eyes to stay glued on the concrete ahead.

"You're just braver," Max added.

Bridger pondered for a moment. *That's his apology?*

But then, he stepped off his board. He looked up at his first mentor, absorbing his words. *That's a lot for him.*

Bridger nodded at Max. Max nodded back.

It was all they needed to say.

Bridger jumped onto his board and pushed off down the concrete bumps. He gained speed as he pumped down the stretch and circled back around to the flat where Max stood.

He bent his knees and jumped into the air, flipped the board beneath him, and landed the varial kickflip body varial.

"Hell yeah!" Max roared with pride. "Let's go!"

Chapter 16

Colors Yet to Come

Soon, August's approaching end brought Montana's smoky season. Gus and Bridger soaked in as many final days of adventure as they could before Gus had to leave for college. With their deepening relationship, skating, and now their expanding board business, the boys' lives had become almost inextricable. Bridger slept over at the cabin so frequently that Dan often had to kindly send him home so Gus could focus on their carpentry. On Gus's days off, the boys swam and kissed in Gus's secret lake behind Dan's property, went whitewater rafting in Yellowstone Park, and rock climbed in Bear Canyon. After delivering Tara Shae her custom skateboard, which she proudly showed off around town, not only did all the skaters in Livingston seem to crave a *SCRAPS* board, but all their families eventually started requesting new furniture as well. With the increased workload in his small shop, Dan started paying Bridger to handle some simple woodworking tasks in addition to focusing on customer interactions to fulfill the surge of new orders. Within a week, Dan promoted Bridger to an official part-time employee because of how effortlessly the boy could sweet-talk both skater kids and elderly couples alike into seeing the "once-in-a-lifetime" value of owning a Shepard original.

When September hit, Gus's final few days in town grew increasingly bittersweet. His father watched Gus woodwork during his last shifts with a mix of pride and sorrow. Tara asked about Gus's upcoming art classes often, trying to get him used to the idea of moving away like she was. Bridger held each hug with Gus a little longer and a little tighter. Everyone was feeling the impact of his inevitable departure.

Gus could feel the oncoming change, too. He tried to savor every small, final sensation: the hot sun on the skatepark's concrete, the whirring wheels rolling across mounds and the clanging of decks on rails, the sweetness of sawdust swirling in the shop, the laughter of his friends. With all of it, Gus kept telling himself, *You're gonna miss this. Remember it now before it's gone.*

The morning Gus had to fly out to Rhode Island, he sat packing his bags in his wooden attic bedroom with Bridger. The lamps were lit low. Calming music played. The boys focused on steadily folding shirts and packing art tools into boxes. Gus added a last piece of clothing to his suitcase and zipped it shut. He handed his backpack to Bridger.

Gus broke the silence first. "Thanks again for helping me pack."

"Of course," Bridger replied softly, taking Gus's bag to the desk that held Dan's computer and some art supplies. The room was full of melancholy warmth. Both boys knew they were going to part soon. Neither of them knew how to say goodbye.

"I spoke with Tara yesterday," Gus said.

"Yeah?" Bridger prompted.

Gus nodded. "She starts her Cali job next week," he said, pushing a smile.

"Rad. That's... great." Bridger nodded, tapping his hand at his side.

He then looked down and saw an RISD pamphlet sticking up from Gus's belongings. He picked up the brochure and flipped through it.

"There's lots of art clubs on your campus," Bridger observed. "No skateparks though."

Gus shrugged. "I'm not sure if I want to join any clubs." He sat down on his bed. "I just want to pass my classes. And... I'm not good at meeting new people."

"What? Nah. Join some," Bridger encouraged gently. "Pretty soon you'll have all new friends."

He put the brochure in Gus's backpack along with some colored pencils. He paused.

"Pretty soon, you won't even have to think about Montana anymore," Bridger added, letting his head fall.

Gus sighed gently. He slid his suitcase from the bed to the ground and caught Bridger's eyes.

"I'm not gonna forget this summer, Bridger," Gus assured him.

His skater boy shrugged. "Seems like everyone's about to have a brand new start." Bridger exhaled sadly. "And I still don't even know my next step."

Gus tilted his head. He stood up to join Bridger by the desk.

"I mean, you didn't know your next steps when you started teaching me how to skate." Gus pressed his shoulder to Bridger's. "And that worked out."

Bridger nodded drearily in return. He walked to sit down on Gus's bed. Gus followed him.

"What am I gonna do without you here?" Bridger breathed. "No one knows me like you do. Not really."

Gus scanned Bridger's eyes. His face wore a sad but grateful pout.

"Then open up more. Let other people get to know the real Bridger," Gus suggested. "I know I like him a lot. Others will, too."

Bridger scoffed. "No one cares that much, trust me. Easier to just go back to kickflips and smoking with the guys."

"They *will* care though," Gus reassured him. "Because the real you... makes *nothing* special."

"I... what?" Bridger chuckled.

"What we said back at the lake." Gus lifted his head up,

remembering. He smiled slowly in contemplation. "This summer could have been terrible. Mom just died, I never got along with Dad, I had nothing to do. But somehow, you taught me how to make every day better. To take a whole lot of nothing and have it become something... memorable," Gus reflected.

The sweet words stuck in the heavy air.

Gus leaned his forehead against the side of Bridger's head. "I'm grateful we made the most of the time we did have."

Bridger placed his hand on Gus's. "I wish we had more."

The boys sat in silence. Bridger pouted again but then leaned over and gave Gus a tender kiss. Gus kissed back. After they parted, Bridger lowered his head. He sighed with a chuckle and looked up.

"You're sure you won't forget about me in that bigger city? At that fancy college?" Bridger joked.

Gus flicked Bridger's chin and smiled. "No. Because for each day of nothing where I push myself to try something wild or new... I'll think of you."

Bridger bit his lip, trying to ward off the grief setting in. He pulled Gus roughly into a hug that he hoped said how much this had all meant to him.

Gus let a tear fall, and Bridger squeezed him harder.

When the boys separated, Bridger looked at Gus deeply.

"Things will be okay... right?" Bridger asked. "With us?"

Gus hesitated. He wanted to immediately say "Of course!" He wanted to say that nothing could ever change what they'd built this summer. But... the truth was, Gus had no idea what would happen next. He had no idea what would happen over breaks or over the summers that awaited. College could change his life for the better, or everything could get worse than it was before April. Suddenly, he was terrified all over again. However, this time, Gus didn't panic. He didn't stay stuck in his own mind. He looked at Bridger, at the boy he fell in love with this summer, and took a deep, calm breath.

Gazing intently into Bridger's eyes, Gus did know two things for certain.

"We'll be okay," Gus promised. "And, I'll be back."

"I... I'll miss you," Bridger said, barely a whisper.

"I'll miss you, too." Gus pulled Bridger in. "So much."

The boys held their final, tearful embrace on Gus's bed.

Gus walked through the cabin for the last time that summer with his backpack and suitcase. Bridger followed behind holding both their skateboards. As Gus passed his mother's newly re-hung *Elk in Forest* painting in the entryway, he paused. He took a second to soak in its enchanting beauty. He glanced around him at the rest of the cabin's walls, at all his mother's favorite pieces that his father had returned to their rightful places. Gus released a slow, satisfied breath he hadn't realized was pent up. That familiar warming comfort he had missed for so long had finally returned to his home. Gus opened the door, and together, Gus and Bridger stepped outside the cabin.

The boys turned to see Dan walking over from locking up the woodshop. He carried a cardboard box and nodded his head at Gus and Bridger.

The smoky Montana air was quiet and somber. The boys lingered on the porch, avoiding their farewell. The Bozeman airport was a forty-minute drive away.

"Let's get a move on." Dan patted his son's shoulder. "We're already runnin' late." He handed the cardboard box to Bridger and grabbed Gus's suitcase.

"I know, I know." Gus hiked up his backpack.

Dan carried Gus's luggage over to his car, popped the trunk, and placed it inside.

Gus turned to Bridger, about to offer a quick hug, but Bridger instead held out Dan's box.

Gus accepted it.

"This is from your dad," Bridger said, "and something small from me."

Gus brightened, surprised. He knew both his father and Bridger weren't exactly gift-givers. He reached to rip open the box.

"Don't open it yet. Wait till you're on your own," Bridger said.

As Bridger stood there before him wearing his new *Shepard's Custom Furniture* T-shirt, Gus marveled at how far they had come. The boys traded tender smiles.

A surge of uncertainty swept over Gus. He felt the pull to kiss Bridger again, one last time. However, it felt too final. Like he wasn't coming back. Gus sighed. He also was still too shy to kiss Bridger with his dad so close by.

Bridger nodded slowly, catching Gus's eyes full of desire. *I want to kiss you, too.*

"Okay," Gus agreed. "I'll wait."

Bridger handed Gus's skateboard painted with mountains to him. He kept his board of flames. The boards that brought them together now had to be separated, too.

Gus didn't want to leave. It was so hard to move his feet.

Bridger sniffled a bit but kept a strong face.

This sorrowful, shared, silent gaze *was* their goodbye.

It dripped with both heartache and love.

Eventually, Gus turned to walk to his father's car. He opened the passenger door and placed the cardboard box in front of the seat.

Before stepping in, Gus twisted to take a final look at the Montana mountains behind the home he grew up in. Their vast magnitude still filled him with awe. They framed his little house that stored so many memories he didn't want to abandon. Gus then looked back at Bridger, still standing on the cabin porch. His subtle sad smile forced Gus to hold back tears. The boys each gave a final small wave.

"You ready?" Dan asked from the driver's side, pausing as he got in.

Gus glanced again at Bridger, who looked down at his feet. Gus could tell he was in agony. So was he.

No, he wasn't ready.

"I, uh... I just..." Gus peered back at Bridger.

Dan followed his son's gaze toward the skater boy at his door. He sighed. He knew this feeling all too well. Parting hurt most when returns weren't guaranteed. Dan observed Gus for a moment from across his car—saw with a wistful ache that his son was yet again taller than he remembered. His little boy had grown up stronger than he could have ever hoped for. In this moment, so many of Dan's old regrets faded away.

"Gus?"

His son looked up.

Dan smiled. "Go say goodbye."

Gus locked eyes with his father. He let out a shaky laugh as a quick tear fell. Gus immediately dropped his backpack and his skateboard and dashed back to the house, back to Bridger.

Gus ran so fast he almost tripped as he leaped to throw his arms around the boy who taught him everything that mattered most.

"Oh!" Bridger winced at first, but then eased into Gus's embrace.

Gus held his chin in the crook of Bridger's shoulder and squeezed as tight as his arms would allow. He didn't want to let go. This was his first real friend, his first real love.

Gus lifted his chin and placed a slow, final kiss upon Bridger's lips. The boy's eyebrows raised, then melted. Bridger reached up to cup Gus's face, making this last kiss count.

When they finally parted lips, Bridger held their hug.

"Goodbye, Gus," he whispered.

Dan let Gus and Bridger have their private farewell and waited inside the car for Gus. Eventually, his son bent down into the vehicle to take his seat and closed the door. The Chevy Blazer pulled out and drove away.

Whenever Dan was driving, Gus often sat alone in the back. But today, he sat in the front passenger seat, right next to his father. For the next few minutes, they both sat in somber silence as they sped down the highway. Gus opened his window and let the last of summer's breeze blow upon his face.

With only an empty road and plenty of time ahead of them, Dan eventually nodded to the cardboard box in Gus's lap.

"Open it," Dan said casually.

"But I'm not alone yet," Gus responded.

"Humpfrh," Dan muttered.

Giving a smiling shake of his head, Gus ripped the tape off the box and gently opened the cardboard wings to find an object wrapped in newspaper. His forehead raised in pleasant surprise as he caught eyes with his father. Dan released the smallest of grins and glanced back at the road. Gus gingerly unfolded the newspaper to find a small pile of wood. At first, Gus was confused until two of the rectangular pieces opened to reveal Dan's parting gift: Gus's old tattered sketchbook that he had ripped up and thrown away, but now restored and strengthened with hardwood covers and each page fully laminated.

Shock, relief, and excitement hit Gus all at once. Dan muttered a laugh as his son reacted.

Gus opened the book to find all his old drawings of Montana nature, animals, skateboards, birds, and Bridger rebound into the new wooden sketchbook. Every ripped-up page, his dad had meticulously taped back together.

Tilting his head, Gus looked fondly at the months of memories as he flipped through the pages. He was surprised by all the little sketches he had forgotten about and, more than that, how much time and care his father must have put into matching together all the scraps of paper to put them back where they belonged. As he skimmed through the restored book, Gus discovered a journey of multiple different sparrows mixed within the summer's sketches that grew more colorful with every page. Gus let a tear fall as he found his favorite last sketch of Bridger, whole again, sunbathing with his rain-soaked cheek.

From his backpack, where he'd pressed it between two art books, Gus pulled out the drawing of his mother that he'd saved. The one he couldn't bring himself to destroy. Dan watched with a nostalgic smile on his face as Gus slipped it in with the one of Bridger. His old sketchbook was forever stronger than it was before.

Gus closed the back cover, and his eyes widened with more curiosity. There, written on the wooden back, was an engraved message from Dan.

> Dear Gus, Never throw away painful memories
> that led to today's joy. A great life is built by
> the moments we refuse to forget.

Gus smiled as he read the words.

He then noticed the rest of the wood he'd lifted from the box was an untouched second sketchbook. Immediately, he flipped to look at the back, pleased to find another engraved message, this one below an embedded picture of his happy, young father and mother.

> This new sketchbook is one your mom never
> got to use. She always dreamed of going
> to art college. Thank you for reminding
> me of her.
>
> Keep drawing.
> Love, Dad

Gus glanced over at his father. The aging man bowed his head mournfully while keeping his eyes on the road.

"There's more..." Dan prompted, gesturing toward the new sketchbook.

Gus opened the wooden cover to the first blank page. Taped there was a postcard, a Polaroid, and a sparrow's feather. The nature-filled Montana postcard offered a simple message:

> I'll never forget my summer
> with you, Bird Boy.

At the bottom was Bridger's signature and the date. August 2003. The Polaroid showed the boys together, laughing up in Gus's room. He immediately chuckled thinking of Bridger and all their nights under both the stars and his twinkling fairy lights. However, as time held, Gus's smile slipped away as bittersweet tears welled in his eyes. That boy changed his life for the better. Truly. Yet, right now, the dreary and regretful memories fading back in were not of his new lover but of the one person who had loved him first.

"I miss Mom so much," Gus shared as a droplet wet his cheek. "I wish she was here right now. I wish she could have met Bridger… There's so much I'll never be able to tell her."

Dan remained stoic in the driver's seat.

Gus held strong, not wanting to weep. The grief always hit him hardest when he pictured his mother's radiant smile and how he'd never see it again. He looked into his sketch of her. Missing her eyes.

"I wish she knew that you and I had this summer together, Dad."

Dan looked out the windshield at the picturesque Montana landscape around them, at all the vivid colors he had taken for granted for so many years. Today, he found them more vibrant than they had ever been.

"Your mother knows, kid." Dan smiled softly. "She knows."

Tears streamed down as Gus looked into the side view mirror to get one final look back at Livingston, Montana, shrinking in the reflection. The portrait of his hometown in the little glass was more stunning than any sketch he had ever drawn.

Gus wiped his cheek.

Mom would have loved this view.

Gus chose, right then, to be grateful for his summer of experiences. The furniture, the escapades, building skateboards, making mistakes, gaining new friends, falling in love with Bridger—everything.

Gus turned forward, plucked the sparrow feather from between his gifts, and twirled it in his fingers. He looked down at his renewed sketchbook with its drawings so colorful they actually looked like the real world around him. For the first time, Gus's drawings matched his reality.

The boy pulled out his colored pencils.

Gus carefully removed the Polaroid of him and Bridger from the new sketchbook and re-taped it to the final page of his old one. Then he began drawing the bright blue sky and evergreen hills beyond the front windshield. Gus glanced up and leaned out his open front passenger window. He wanted to ensure he made the most of all the blending colors before him. Finally, he understood how they all worked in harmony.

Gus's last addition to his drawing was something simple. He sketched two young red sparrows flying in the distant wind. He knew both birds could see all the colors yet to come over the big mountains that stood in their way.

I did it, Mom.

I finally made some art I'm proud of.

I can't wait to share it with you one day...

As Dan's Chevy rounded the curvy bend facing a new visage of magnificent magenta mountains and emerald forests stretching far and wide, Gus cracked a confident smile.

He pulled out his mother's empty wooden sketchbook and turned to its first, fresh page.

Gus Shepard couldn't wait to draw something bright and new.

Author's Note

Scraps began as a <u>short film</u> Ryan and I wrote, then produced. A small story about first gay crushes on straight boys, skateboarding, woodworking, and the weight of growing up in a place that doesn't always understand you. To our surprise, that little film resonated with a dazzling number of people—it spread across the internet, played at many film festivals, and connected us with a community of skaters, artists, and other queer people who saw themselves in Gus and Bridger.

That's when we knew this story wasn't over.

This *Scraps* novel expands on what the short film started, diving deeper into Gus and Bridger's relationship, their backstories, their fears, and the messy, beautiful ways we figure out who we are as young queer people. And this is only the beginning—*Scraps* is also in development as a feature film to begin production in June 2025.

Thank you for reading, for skating, and for believing in love, in second chances, and in this story.

If you want to follow the journey, find us at:
<u>@scraps_movie</u>
<u>@matthewfrancisj</u>
<u>@rye_nordin</u>

Acknowledgments

Writing a book is never a solo act, and *Scraps* wouldn't exist without some incredible people.

To **Ryan Nordin**, who was there from the start, shaping this story alongside me—this book is as much yours as it is mine.

To my **family and friends**, who supported my early-morning writing sessions at 3:00 a.m. and listened to me talk about Gus and Bridger like they were real people.

To the **skateboarding community,** for inspiring this story and reminding us why skateboarding is more than just a sport—it's freedom, expression, and rebellion all at once.

To the my fellow **LGBTQ+ people**. I strive to represent us well and tell our stories. Thank you for being my found family.

To my **readers and viewers**, especially those who fell in love with our short film—thank you for proving that stories like this matter.

To our **short film cast and crew**, you all first brought our *Scraps* story to life and made the world recognize our vision and the impact it could have.

To **Samantha Zaboski,** our novel editor, who helped sand our rough skateboarding story into a sleek, polished masterpiece.

And finally, to anyone who's ever felt like they didn't belong—this one's for you.

—Matthew Francis

About the Authors

MATTHEW FRANCIS (1995)- Matthew is an American chef, writer, producer, and director born in Duluth, Minnesota. Before graduating from the Culinary Institute of America in 2016, Matthew worked in various restaurants around the USA. He has always been a deep lover of queer romance and sci-fi/fantasy stories.

Matthew has directed over 4,100 recipe videos for multiple major media companies including *BuzzFeed Tasty*, Dotdash Meredith's *Food & Wine*, *Eating Well*, *Allrecipes*, *Better Homes & Gardens*, *Serious Eats*, *Southern Living*, and more. *Scraps* is a continuation of the 2025 short film of the same name. The *Scraps* feature film is currently in pre-production.

In his free time, Matthew is always writing new stories, cooking up delicious meals, playing in local queer sports leagues, or slaying monsters in Dungeons & Dragons. He hopes to continue growing his career in food media and writing diverse queer stories of every genre. He wants his work to impact real people's lives and support voices that are craving to be noticed.

RYAN NORDIN (1999)- Ryan is an American director and screenwriter. He got his start working as a visual effects artist for brands like Samsung, Oakley, and ESPN before transitioning to directing. Ryan is based in Los Angeles and is a founding member of Mission Ranch, a production company that has grown to a team of fifteen. Ryan recently directed commercials for Pepsi, Wrangler, and MVMT, and the documentary *Vincint: There Will be Tears,* an LGBTQ+ documentary featuring musician Vincint Cannady shot on Super 8mm film and screened at Outfest LA. Ryan hopes his work will help shed a light on underrepresented communities, telling stories for change.